A MORE WICKED SEA

BY EM BROWN

A MORE WICKED SEA

CHAPTER ONE

I n the cabin of her ship, Captain Marinette La Croix sat in her favorite Edwardian armchair. Its every quality, from the patterned jacquard upholstery to the ornately carved skirt and baluster legs to the gilded urn finials, was masculine.

But not nearly as masculine as the man who stood before her, Harry Edge, formerly her slave and now her first mate. Dispensing with a coat, he wore only a long waistcoat over a shirt that had its sleeves cut off. She tried not to salivate at the sight of his muscular arms and think of the taut ridges of his chest and torso. There was not an inch of him that did not command her desire. Even the hook that took the place of his right hand oddly compelled her.

Predicting what he came to tell her, she said, "The men are restless."

"Aye," Harry acknowledged. "We've been many days at sea without a raid, and the rum be gone."

"They are impatient. As most men are."

"Perhaps a few days at a port with some wenches would please them."

She eyed him carefully. "And what say you? Are you displeased?"

"Only if my captain is displeased."

She waved off his answer. "You've no complaints, I suppose, if you have ten thousand pieces of eight as you once claimed."

"They exist."

She had barely believed him the first time he had made mention of his hidden treasure and used the promise of it to lure her into spreading her legs beneath him.

"But half belongs to my brother," he continued, "and both of us are required to access it. The chest has two locks. I have one key, and he the other."

Harry rarely mentioned his older brother, though she had heard the name of Drake Edge on occasion at various ports of call. He commanded *The Curse of Neptune* and kept mostly to terrorizing the British colonies of Georgia and the Carolinas.

La Croix stood up. The hour was late, and she was prepared for bed. She had only to wrap her

2

hair, which she wore in dozens of queues with small shells woven into the braids.

"A few more days," she said. "If by then, we've not sighted quarry, then I will consider a stop."

The shirt she wore barely hung past her groin, and she noted Harry's gaze linger upon her smooth legs. His icy blue eyes appeared to soften, and she knew his desire. She tried to dismiss her responding arousal. It had not been wise to allow her first mate between her legs. After years of bedding only whores, she had allowed a man into her bed. Though no one in her crew knew of her and Harry, she had to be careful. Despite being the daughter of the dreaded pirate Baron La Croix, being a woman and a captain was no easy task. She could show no weakness.

"The men have gone off to bed," Harry said. "Their merrymaking be limited in the absence of rum."

She lifted her chin, understanding the proposal behind his statement. "What of the watch?"

"Glad to be in his hammock. I offered to take his shift."

She raised her brows. She should make him fulfill this duty. A few hours in the crow's nest might cure him of his presumption.

But already she had the sense that sleep would elude her if she did not address the lust simmering within her. Like her men, she felt restless. She had not taken Harry into her bed since she had punished him for disregarding her directive during their last raid. Pleasuring herself, however, only provided temporary satiation. Fondling or using the dildo upon herself could not compare to a hard and passionate fuck. Even after bringing herself to spend, sometimes several times in one night, she would have to face Harry the following day. One look from him sent her hunger flaring. His look, reminding her of a wolf presented with raw meat, made no qualms of his desire to devour her.

"You expecting to be invited into my bed?" she asked him as she closed the distance between them.

"You want me in your bed, Captain," he replied.

She shook her head. Such arrogance.

He lowered his head and spoke low near her ear. "I seen the way you look at me. I can *scent* your desire."

Her breath skittered.

He straightened, speaking as if commenting upon the winds. "You hunger for my cock. That dildo of yours cannot compare."

He knew she used one, did he? She attempted to slice him down a peg with her response. "It be larger than your cock, knave."

Unperturbed, he wrapped an arm about her and drew her into him till her body pressed against the bulge in his crotch. "But does it pleasure you as much as my cock can?"

Heat immediately pooled beneath her belly.

"I might take you into my bed," she said, drawing out each word, "if you'll be bound to it."

His lips tightened in a small frown, but he said, "As you wish, Captain."

She pulled from him. "Strip to the buff, then."

He removed his sword belt and pistol holder. As she did, he kept his weapons about him at all times. Like her, he trusted no one. As he began to disrobe, she admired every inch he laid bare. His days in the sun gave his body a bronze hue that she preferred much more to the common pale Englishman. When he stood completely naked before her, knowing that she gloried in his beauty, she opened a drawer in the sideboard and pulled out several cords of rope.

"Upon my bed then," she instructed. "On your back."

He did as she bid, lying still as she began to tie each limb to its own bedpost. After she had bound his ankles and the arm with his hook, she licked her lips at the sight of his strong form stretched across her bed. Crawling next to him, she bent down and kissed him, taking her time to explore his mouth with her own. And as her tongue slid into his mouth, she wrapped the second rope about his other wrist. Disengaging from his mouth, she made a knot in the rope. As tight as the bond was, she would not be surprised if he managed to wrestle free. He had done so the last time she had him tied to her bed. She sat back to assess his reaction, daring him to test the bindings and risk punishment. When he made no complaint or movement, she reached for his stiffened rod of desire. He sucked in a breath as she stroked the tip, playing with the drop of liquid that she found there. She slid her hand down the shaft, appreciating its size and shape.

As she stroked his warm veined rod, she watched his every breath and the gleam in his eyes as lust rose higher in his body. He had shown no dismay at being bound and rendered defenseless.

As when he was her slave, he had submitted to her every whim, but she doubted that he relished a state of powerlessness any more than a tiger would want to be caged. Once more the desire to test his fortitude burned within her. She lowered her head, teasingly close to his cock. He shifted slightly but resisted shoving his hips up at her. She licked his tip, making him gasp. She looked up to meet his cool blue gaze.

"Be wanting something?" she taunted.

"You," he returned with his icy heat, as if he were speaking to someone he intended to kill, but she knew it was his ardor that spoke with such conviction. She shivered.

"Bent over the edge of the bed with my cock pounding into you," he added.

She frowned at this test of her dominance. He would pay for that. Her cunnie, however, received the vision differently, growing warm and wet.

"You want to fuck me, eh?" she replied.

As if he knew he had overstepped, he said nothing at first, then answered, undaunted, "I know it would give my captain great pleasure."

A decent save, she thought to herself.

"And what of your pleasure?" she mused aloud.

"It serves yours."

"Indeed? You would not attempt to spend before I did?"

"When have I ever?"

She planted a light kiss upon his erection. "No man has such forbearance."

He did not dispute her, but replied, "You will want my cock for your own purposes."

"I have other means of spending."

"That you have, but not in ways that could best my cock."

"Are you so certain?"

"I am not the one at risk of being fooled here."

She raised her brows despite the truth of what he said. She did favor his cock, but she did not appreciate his arrogance. Wanting to provide him a set-down, she playfully licked his tip, then swirled her tongue over the crown, before sinking down upon him, inch by inch. A low groan rumbled in his throat. Slowly, she bobbed up and down his cock till his hips moved slightly in concert. She sucked him hard, making him grunt, then came off him in time to see his lashes flutter. If she wanted, she could make him spend. She could emerge the victor in this challenge, but she preferred to torment him first.

His breath was uneven but his countenance remained stoic. It would not remain so for long, she determined.

CHAPTER TWO

L a Croix climbed off the bed. Harry watched her, his eyes never straying from her form as she crossed the room and retrieved a candle from her table. Patiently, she returned to her prey. How glorious his muscular form looked strapped to her bed, his thick arousal standing at proud attention, saluting her. She sat down beside his hip and held up the candle, studying the flicker of the flame before hovering it over his groin. Slowly, she tilted the candle. He inhaled sharply as the melted wax hit his pelvis. She brought the candle over his cock and looked to see stoicism in his countenance. He knew what was coming, and it seemed his hardened expression even dared her to proceed.

The hot liquid spilled onto his cock. He strained against the ropes. Grabbing him to keep his shaft perpendicular to his body, she moved the candle even closer and coated his tip. He seemed to bite back an oath.

After setting aside the candle on a small table

beside the bed, she pulled off her shirt. His eyes lighted upon seeing her bared body. She cradled her breasts and caressed them, playing with her nipples, closing her eyes and enjoying the feel of her own hands on her body. She could feel Harry's cock bob against her. He grunted as she ground herself against his wax-encrusted shaft. She bent forward until her breasts touched his chest, and then she slowly made her way down his body, allowing her breasts to caress him as she did.

Coming to his cock, she picked off the wax that had hardened on his tip. She spat into her hand and rubbed her spittle along his shaft before placing him between her breasts. His eyes widened as she squeezed the orbs about his length. She moved up and down, enjoying the sound of his breath quickening. His cock was so hard, so ripe for fucking...

But she resisted the urge to sit herself down on his manhood and instead crawled back up to his chest. Lightly, she caressed the smooth planes of his pectorals, relishing the firmness of his chest beneath her fingertips and palms. She passed her fingers over his nipples, hardening them further. He grunted. Lowering her head, she took his nipple into her mouth and gently sucked. His back arched. She sucked harder. He grunted. She bit down. He gasped. She looked up to ascertain if he enjoyed the attentions upon his nipples. She suspected not for he frowned. Good.

She went back to nibbling on one nipple, then licked the other before biting down hard enough to make him release an oath. Her cunnie throbbed in response, and she intensified her feasting. For the next several minutes, she devoured his nipples, greedy for his grunts and ragged breaths.

"S'blood," he cursed when she bit down hard enough to draw blood.

She applied her hands next, twisting his nipples till he grimaced in pain. The muscle along his jaw tightened as she rolled the nubs between her thumbs and fingers. She gave his nipples a quick lick before resuming the pinching and twisting, not letting up till she knew the soreness in his nipples would last through the morning. She could feel herself growing wet as his entire body tensed in pain. Marvelous how such small points on the body could have such an effect. He had even started to sweat.

"You want I should stop, Harry?" she teased, wondering if he now regretted coming into her cabin.

He drew in a breath before replying, "The more you torment me, the more I desire to fuck you, Captain."

Not expecting this response, her mouth dropped. His words made her ache between the legs, ache for him to fill the void there. His words were a weapon she had to disable. Reaching over to the table, she grabbed the kerchief she used to wrap her hair before bed.

"If you wish me to stop," she informed him, "you will have to beg it of me."

"Begging not be something I do. Not even when Chacón severed my hand and rubbed salt into my bleeding stump, did I once beg."

"Then it will matter not to you to take this gag." She fit the kerchief between his lips and wound it behind his head. "But should you want to beg, you must do so with your eyes."

She reached once more for the candle, holding it closer to his body this time so that the wax would have less time to cool before striking his flesh. She dripped wax over his chest and a nipple. He inhaled loudly through his nose. She made his body a canvas, painting him with pools of wax, splattering his chest, his abdomen, the hairs at his groin, his legs, and his scrotum.

Several times she glanced into his eyes. At times they seemed to flare with emotion, but not once did they beg.

When there was nothing left of the candle, her arousal could no longer be denied, could no longer resist this fine specimen of man, a strong feral beast tied to her bed, helpless and at her mercy. She reached down and picked his sword belt off the floor. Straddling him once more, she fit the belt around his neck. Holding the belt, she began to grind herself along his cock, her wetness making his hardness slick. This time when he grunted, she knew it was in pleasure.

A small shift in angle and his cock slid inside her. She closed her eyes and stilled herself, savoring the hardness throbbing inside her, her cunnie no longer empty. Her cunnie flexed about him, making his cock jerk. She sank herself deeper, her toes curling at the exquisite sensation of being filled by him. Urgency soon replaced any desire to relish the joining of their bodies. She began to pump herself up and down his shaft while tugging on the belt that enclosed his throat. She pulled tighter. His eyes widened as the flow of air was cut. His body strained against his bonds. She let the belt loosen. He gulped his breaths as best he could with the kerchief in his mouth. His reprieve was short-lived as she yanked the belt tight once more and bore down harder on his cock. He started to tremble, his limbs shaking in need of air. Seeing the veins protrude in his neck and the desperation in his face sent her over the pinnacle into spasms of pleasure. She cried out as wetness streamed from her. She fell forward, gasping for breath as her sex quivered around Harry's member.

Mon Dieu. Mon Dieu.

After several minutes, she stirred herself. She had lost track of Harry and idly wondered if she might have killed him while in throes of ecstasy.

But he was not dead. His cock was hard as ever, and lust still burned in his eyes. He was primed for the final blow.

"I will release your bonds," she said, "that you may go."

He stared at her, perhaps not believing that she intended to dismiss him.

"Captain?" he inquired after she had removed her kerchief from his mouth.

"You must tend to the watch," she reminded him as she reached to undo the ropes from his wrists.

As soon as he had a free hand, he grabbed her, yanking her to him. "I let you choke the air from me."

Seeing his eyes flash, her face mere inches from his, her pulse quickened, but she kept her nerves in check. "Aye. And?"

Once more she was aware that she taunted an animal of prey. A muscle along his jaw rippled.

"You may go, Harry," she reiterated.

For a tense moment she knew not what he would do next. Even with his ankles still bound, he could find a way for force himself upon her. Her ardor would not balk if he did. Indeed, it stirred at the prospect of being held down by him. But she had given him an order, and she would see it through.

He released her, displeasure writ upon his physiognomy. While she tended to her hair, smug with his compliance, that he had little choice but to obey her lest he wished to suffer the consequences, she watched him untie the bonds at his ankles. He yanked the belt off his neck and grabbed his articles from the floor. His cock still protruded long and hard, but he pulled his breeches over it and put on his waistcoat. She pulled the bedclothes over her nudity and watched him stride out of her cabin. She knew he would think twice now about coming into her cabin for a fuck without prompting.

As she lay her head upon the pillow and closed her eyes, she settled into a fitful slumber, aware that there may be a price to pay for going too far with a wolf.

CHAPTER THREE

"**S**he be a pretty sloop. As fine a sight as cunnie," remarked Poirer as he peered through the spyglass. "French built, I'll wager."

An older French man who had served with the Baron La Croix, Poirer had expected to become her first mate till she chose to elevate Harry instead. To her surprise, Poirer had chosen to remain with the *Bloody Baron,* and though she knew he chafed at having to take orders from an Englishman, after his initial complaint to her, he had kept his grousing to the French members of her crew.

Standing upon the poop deck with Harry beside her, Marinette received the spyglass from her pilot and gave orders for the *Bloody Baron* to draw closer. A bright blue sky made it a fine day for plunder.

"Which flag shall we hoist?" asked Poirer.

A Dutch flag was less likely to offend, but Marinette waited for Harry, who continued to study their intended quarry through the spyglass.

"Spanish," Harry confirmed.

Marinette gave the orders and watched her crew ready the flag of red and yellow. She drew in a long breath to stall the anticipation stirring in her body. They had been over a sennight without a prospect, but it appeared they would soon reap the rewards of their wait.

"Cannon crews ready!" she commanded when they drew within striking distance.

"Cannons ready," came the response.

Beside her, Harry stiffened. She looked over to see his jaw set firmly as he continued to look through the spyglass. She waited for him to speak. Did the number of cannons on the sloop concern him?

"It is one of Chacón's ships," he revealed.

Receiving the spyglass from Harry, she confirmed for herself the coat of arms upon the flag flying beneath that of Spain. She glanced at Harry but could not discern what emotion he felt.

"Shall we take her with as much bloodshed as possible?" she asked.

He looked down at his hook before meeting her eye.

"It shall be as *you* wish, Captain."

"Then kill as many men as you wish."

A faint grin touched the corner of his lips. "Aye, Captain."

She acknowledged the appreciation in his eyes with a nod before heading down to ready herself. She put a coat over her customary shirt, waistcoat and breeches. Her cutlass was already strapped to her, and she added a loaded pistol.

The Spanish colors flying from the mast of the *Bloody Baron* allowed them to approach the sloop. Through the spyglass, she could see the captain of the sloop studying her ship. The captain turned to his first mate and asked several questions. The latter shook his head and shrugged his shoulders. Undoubtedly, they did not recognize her ship and wondered who she could be. She smiled to herself. They would soon find out.

The Spanish captain knew something was amiss. The galleon began to turn away from them.

"Hoist the Jolly Roger," she ordered.

The Spanish flag came down, and up went the skull with a sword through it. Realizing they had indeed been duped, the captain of the sloop quickly ordered his men to prepare the cannons. But the *Bloody Baron* was ready first.

"Send a warning shot across her bow!"

A few seconds later, a cannon threw out a twenty-four pounder, the massive cannon jutting back with the force of the release. La Croix watched as the ball landed far afield of the target.

"Cowards," La Croix muttered, noting the galleon attempting to flee. "Take out her sails!"

Cannon spat out the chain shot, some hurling double-ended bar shot to rip through the sails. The barrage shredded the main and top sails.

"There be quite the number of soldiers aboard her," Harry noted of the men in uniform scrambling to load their firearms.

Realizing it could not outrun the *Bloody Baron*, the galleon began to angle itself in a better position to return fire. Her cannon shutters flew open to reveal the sixteen pounders behind them.

"Grapeshot!" La Croix hollered.

The *Bloody Baron* released an explosion of metal and glass at the galleon, the debris taking out several men as it peppered the deck. Her men began to stomp the deck and pound the ship with their fists, chanting "Blood! Blood! Blood!"

Her crew and the soldiers aboard the galleon exchanged gunfire. The galleon returned fire, blowing a hole in the side of the *Bloody Baron*, but the latter was close enough for La Croix to give out the order to cast the boarding hooks over the sides. Her men were well-experienced in the enterprise, and the big metal hooks flew from the Baron's deck and onto the galleon to pull the two ships together.. More gunfire was exchanged with men on both sides falling beneath the spray of bullets. La Croix, a pistol in each hand, exchanged a look with Harry. She could feel his excitement in her own loins.

The ships listed and creaked as the *Baron* pulled the galleon closer.

La Croix shouted, "Take her now, lads!"

Boarding planks went over the sides and she led her crew over and onto the galleon through a spray of bullets from the frontline of soldiers. Harry always led the way. He seemed to have no fear of death, and she and her men believed he had to be half mad. Behind him were two of her bravest men: Noah, a young runaway slave she had rescued from dying in a crow's cage, and Baako, a large man her father had purchased at a slave auction.

La Croix aimed at a solider in the second row, blasting him before he could fire, turning his face into a mist of red. Her second shot glanced off the shoulder of a soldier. Her rounds dispensed with, she turned next to her cutlasses. She clashed with a Spaniard wielding a saber. The man looked upon her with surprise, then relief. He was certain of victory.

It would spell his defeat.

Their blades connected several times before she allowed the man to knock one of her cutlasses loose from her hand. For a second, he watched it clatter to the deck. She lunged at him with her other cutlass and drove it into his gut. His eyes widened and his mouth dropped open in horror. She pushed her blade in deeper before pulling it out. Blood poured from him as he fell to his knees. She picked up her other cutlass and turned to see Harry slice through a man's neck with his hook.

Where was the captain? she wondered. Was he such a coward that he would not fight beside his men?

"Captain!" Harry shouted.

She turned. A blade sliced into her arm. As she stumbled, Harry ran at her assailant with his sword in hand and his hook poised to strike. Her assailant attempted to parry the attack, but Harry was much stronger and drove his sword into the man's chest. The tip of the sword emerged on the other side. Adjusting his grip upon his sword,

Harry twisted it into the man's flesh. After Harry drew out his sword, the man crumpled to the deck on his back. His body was already going into shock but Harry plunged his sword into the man's right eye socket. Remembering how Harry had beaten the sod who had attempted to rape her, La Croix shook her head. His bloodlust ran unnecessarily high at times. But she would allow him his revenge upon Chacón's ship.

Harry came to La Croix and turned her around to examine the wound on the back of her arm.

"A surface cut," he assessed.

She nodded. She had had worse wounds.

"It be but a matter of time. Stand aside. I shall see it done."

"And give my men reason to think me weak? *Non*."

He knew she would receive further argument as insubordination. Weapons in hands, they returned to the fray. Gradually, her men overcame the crew of the galleon. One by one, the Spaniards surrendered. Her father would be proud, La Croix thought to herself. He hated the Spanish. Not having had the experience her father had, she preferred to hate the English more. Granted, the only man to have had her cunnie in more than five years was one of that dreaded creed, but Harry was a pirate with no allegiance to country.

"Where be the captain?" Harry asked.

"Mayhap hiding in his cabin," she replied.

Harry loaded his pistol, then extracted his sword from his latest kill. La Croix sheathed a cutlass and reloaded her pistols as well. They went in search of the captain.

Coming upon two sentries guarding the captain's quarters, Harry fired his first shot, finding his mark in the man's heart. He fell back against the wall. Harry's superior marksmanship never failed to impress her. She handed him her other pistol. A bullet from the other sentry sailed between them. Harry fired, hitting the sentry in the leg. La Croix did not doubt that it was the accuracy of her pistol, and not Harry's aim, that was at fault.

Still upright, the sentry turned to his bayonet, attempting to stab Harry with it. La Croix slashed her cutlass against the man's neck. Even with blood spurting from him, the sentry attempted to attack Harry, who easily knocked away the Spaniard's rifle.

"The captain must be inside for the man to

persist so," Harry said after the sentry finally succumbed to his wounds.

Harry and La Croix reloaded their pistols before kicking the cabin doors open. Sure enough, they came upon the Spanish captain.

"*La misericordia!*" the older Spaniard cried out.

"Sink me," Harry said for behind the captain stood two women.

One was dressed in the finery of a lady, her hair in a coiffure save for a few curly tendrils that framed a countenance with large, dark eyes and long lashes. Of olive complexion, she appeared twenty years in age, perhaps younger. The other woman, dressed in a much plainer gown, must have been her maid.

"*Hablas ingles?*" La Croix tried.

"A little," the captain replied. He turned to Harry, "Mercy, *por favor.* Please. Take thee ship. But *las señoras*—please spare them."

Harry smirked. "If mercy be what you want, you ask it of the wrong person. *She's* the captain."

The captain furrowed his brow, glancing between Harry and La Croix as if trying to understand the jest. "*El? Es El Capitan?*"

"*Ella. La Capitana,*" Harry corrected.

The eyes of the captain as well as the women widened with disbelief. The captain continued to address Harry, "*Hay mucho dinero sí no les haces daño.*"

"*Eres estúpido?* Bloody dolt." Harry turned to La Croix. "You want I should kill them all now, Captain?"

The younger woman stepped forward and spoke to La Croix. "*La Capitana,* my father is *un hombre muy importante*—important."

Harry narrowed his eyes at her and gazed upon her, perplexed. "Have we met?"

She returned a quizzical look. "I think no."

Of a sudden, Harry paled. "...Chacón."

"You know my name?"

"Your name?"

The Spanish captain said, "Chacón, he is Governor of Cuba."

"I know that," Harry growled.

La Croix raised her brows. "And her father is he?"

"Yes, I am Isabella Chacón," said the young woman, lifting her chin, though La Croix knew she would not wear the name with such pride if she knew who she faced.

"The Governor will reward for her safe

arrival," added the ship's captain.

La Croix had not studied the logs to see what manner of inventory the ship carried, but she did not doubt that the best possession stood before her. Nevertheless, she knew that one of the reasons Harry remained a pirate was because he sought revenge on the man who had taken his hand.

"She is yours," La Croix declared to Harry. "You wish a quick or slow death for her?"

Isabella and the Spanish captain gasped. The maid, who perhaps understood no English, only continued to tremble in fear.

Harry studied Isabella till her cheeks burned with his scrutiny. He scratched his chin in thought. "Neither."

"You want only to ransom her?"

His upper lip curled. "Before we ransom her, I wish to take that which would be most precious to Chacón."

The ship's captain stepped in front of Isabella, extending a protective arm. "*Desalmado!*"

"I, the fiend?" Harry returned. He shoved his hook into the man's face. "I'll gladly exchange Chacón's daughter for my hand."

The man looked horrified.

Isabella shook her head. "No. You—*asesinaste a un hombre*. My father would not—you must have killed someone."

"A fair thought. But if I lost a part of my body every time I killed a man, there should be none of me left."

La Croix sucked in her breath, unsure that she liked Harry's proposal. She understood that the taking of Isabella's maidenhead could provoke even greater anguish than her death, while netting a ransom to boot, but here was yet another instance of an Englishman exerting his dominance. While part of her was grateful that the Baron La Croix had returned to purchase her and her mother from the plantation owner he had sold them to initially, had provided her mother a house and funds, and taken her onto his ship when her mother passed away of malaria, she also hated her father. She hated that she was the bastard offspring of rape.

But she had granted Isabella to Harry. Could she take back his means of revenge?

CHAPTER FOUR

The Spanish beauty, her wrists tied behind her back, stray black locks protruding from her coiffure, trembled, but defiance flared from her eyes. As if he found such bravado quaint, Harry sneered. He grasped her jaw tightly and lifted her chin.

"You've the same arrogant bearing as your father," he snarled into her face.

"R-Remove your dirty hand from me," she replied.

Harry blinked several times before turning to La Croix, who had taken a seat in her chair and was wiping the blood off her sword. Having had her arm bandaged by her ship's doctor, she wore a loose shirt.

"Hear that?" he asked her. "Me hand be dirty."

Releasing Isabella, he examined his hand, marked by drying blood. He smeared the back of his hand upon the bodice of Isabella's gown, staining the yellow satin. Her lower lip dropped. No doubt she had never been treated in such fashion. Rather, she was more likely accustomed to being revered by men, placed upon a pedestal to be admired by all.

"That better, love?" Harry asked. "Or would you prefer my other 'hand'?"

He pressed his hook to the side of her face. Her bosom rose and fell with quickened breaths.

"You can thank your father for this."

Unable or not wanting to meet his gaze, she lowered her thick lashes. She shivered when he slid the metal along her jaw and beneath her chin.

La Croix, recalling all the intimate parts of her that the hook had touched, shifted in her seat. She lay her sword across the armrests and put down the linen to see what else Harry might do and how Isabella would act. La Croix could scent the latter's fear, but the young woman was not as afraid as she ought to be.

Harry lowered both his gaze and hook to her décolletage. He picked at the small pink bow in the center. The hook grazed the flesh above, the orbs nicely swollen thanks to the tight corset that also served to narrow her waist.

"Chacón took my hand," Harry murmured as he leaned in closer, invading her space, "and now I intend to take something of value from him."

"*Por favor*. Please. My father will pay—*mucho dinero*—for me."

Harry took a deep inhale of her sent. "I'm sure he would for a daughter as lovely as you, but money be not what I'm after."

"A pardon? A letter of marque?"

He fit the hook into her cleavage, the point of it poking beneath her décolletage. He yanked, ripping the bodice. To Marinette's surprise, Isabella did not scream, though she was visibly surprised and shaken.

"Please...I am to be married."

"Indeed? Who be the lucky man?"

"The son of the governor...of..."

"What a prize he be receiving from Chacón. Surely a lovelier virgin could not be had. You are a virgin, aye?"

She responded with some indignation, "*Por supuesto!*"

He smirked. "Shall we be certain?"

Her eyes widened. Knowing what was to come, Marinette grew warm. It was a pity the señorita was unlikely to enjoy herself. She was not likely to appreciate how good it felt to have his cock buried inside her cunt. Isabella tried to flee, but he caught her around the waist and tossed her onto the bed.

"Let us see your virginal loins," he said as he tried to throw up her skirts.

She kicked and thrashed, but he caught an ankle and yanked her over the edge of the bed. He delivered a hard slap to her face, momentarily stunning her. He threw her skirts and petticoats over her waist, baring her pelvis.

"What lovely down we have here," he grinned as he palmed her dark curls below. "I think your betrothed would like this very much."

She whimpered and renewed her struggles. Entranced, Marinette watched Isabella's back arch and her legs of alabaster do their best to push herself away from Harry, but he pinned her to the bed with his stronger, heavier body. He swirled his fingers in the hair at her mound before dipping lower. She gasped loudly and turned her head away from Harry, her cheeks reddening.

"Very nice indeed," he murmured as he felt her flesh.

Isabella furrowed her brow as Harry stroked her.

"Well, well," Harry said, "you're fair wet, my dear."

Withdrawing his hand, he displayed his

fingers glistening with her moisture before her eyes, which she promptly shut.

How was that possible? Marinette wondered. She had heard whores complain of dryness with the men they bedded. Of course, she had never heard such complaints of Harry. Was it possible even a woman such as Isabella could not be immune to him either?

"Perhaps we are not as innocent as we seem?" Harry wondered aloud. "Perhaps it be a dream of yours to be ravished by a pirate?"

Isabella knit her brows more tightly together. Harry returned his hand between her legs. Her lips parted as he resumed stroking.

"Is that what you wish, love? To be pleasured by a wicked, dirty pirate?"

A faint groan escaped her as Harry plied the nub presently betraying her.

"Does your father know what a naughty wench he has for a daughter?" he teased.

Her eyes remained closed and her body still, but she emitted a louder moan.

He grinned. "That be the spot, eh?"

After several minutes, La Croix could see Isabella's breathing had grown erratic. She wondered what thoughts went through the woman's head. Was she trying to resist the arousal Harry stirred? Was she both excited and disgusted by him? Was she dismayed to discover her own licentiousness?

Harry turned to La Croix. "Did you know a whore to lay beneath such refinement?"

La Croix did not return an answer. Jealousy now burned alongside her lust, oddly enhancing the latter. She could not resist the carnal response at seeing Harry impose his will upon the maiden, at how Isabella's body responded to his caresses despite her better judgment. But La Croix would sooner he dispense with his revenge and merely ransom the *salope*.

Isabella alternated between gasps and little cries. He caressed her with surprising gentleness and patience till Marinette was tempted to tell him to get on with it.

"*Dios mío...*" she uttered between harsh breaths. "Ahhh...!"

Small spasms shook her body. Her legs jerked. And then a long sigh passed through parted lips before her body relaxed onto the bed.

Harry withdrew his hand and sucked her moisture from his fingers.

"Quite a tasty virgin," he said.

La Croix rolled her eyes. She cursed. The bedclothes were likely wet from the juices of the *connasse*. She would make Harry wash them to ensure they would not smell of the other woman.

"And now the main repast."

Tucking his hook beneath her chin, the point pressed at her throat, he pushed himself up to unbutton his fall.

This jolted Isabella to life. "My father will have your head if you do this. He will search—he will hunt you, and he will kill you."

Her threat fell on idle ears.

"I would expect no less for the taking of his daughter's maidenhead," he replied. "Yours be worth its weight in gold."

Her scream split the air. At last, Marinette thought with satisfaction. She put aside her cutlass and nestled a hand between her own thighs. A small part did pity the woman, but there were women whose fates were far worse, who knew no pleasure before they were raped, La Croix's mother among them. What had Isabella done to deserve better treatment than others of her sex simply because she was born into wealth and breeding? La Croix could not even imagine the sort of privileged life Isabella led. But such an

36

inequities were now better balanced through Harry.

He buried himself in Isabella, who started to sob. La Croix rubbed her crotch, her breeches growing damp, as she watched Harry thrust and withdraw. She wanted to be where Isabella lay, speared on Harry's cock. For a moment, she imagined lying beside Isabella with Harry taking turns between them. The vision both titillated and sickened.

Grabbing her hips, Harry pumped himself into Isabella, whose cries had settled into whimpers.

Fuck her harder, La Croix silently urged as her own cunnie ached to be filled.

Isabella's eyes rolled toward the back of her head. Over and over Harry thrust himself into her slender feminine form. Though the senorita had not the alabaster complexion of British women, Marinette was conscious of her own darkness. She wondered if Harry preferred the paleness of a women more like his kind. Surely their coloring was a mark of beauty in his eyes? Born with a darker complexion, Marinette had only become darker with her days in the sun. She had never carried a parasol in her life.

Did Harry even consider her comely at all, Marinette wondered of herself. Or might he even find her homely, so homely that he, no stranger to perversion, could not help but be aroused by it?

Filled with envy and anger, Marinette rubbed herself harder, her eyes narrowing at Harry, trying to ascertain how much he enjoyed being buried in Isabella. *Get on it with it, you bloody bastard.*

She knew that Harry possessed remarkable endurance, but surely he cared only for his pleasure. Then why did he take his time? Did he intend to see that Isabella spent?

To La Croix's disconcertion, Harry reached a hand between his body and Isabella's to fondle her clitoris. The senorita's lips parted further.

"Halt!" La Croix was tempted to bark. She did not like the swirl of jealousy and arousal inside her. She had never felt the former sentiment in regards *a man*, let alone at the same time as the latter sentiment.

Isabella gave a small cry and a shudder. The wench had spent. La Croix determined she would make Harry pay for that and for soiling the bedclothes with Isabella's blood.

He shoved his hips harshly into Isabella few more times before pulling out his cock. Isabella turned her head away from Harry. La Croix took some satisfaction in seeing large tears, of pain and shame, glistening from the senorita's eyes.

But why did Harry not spend? she wondered.

She received her answer when he turned his gaze to her, the smolder setting her arousal further ablaze.

It was her turn.

CHAPTER FIVE

"I've raised the mast," Harry said, fixing her with a stare that weakened her knees. "Time to drop your sails, Captain, for a sweet and wet wind blows!"

"Take off my boots first, knave," La Croix returned.

Grabbing Isabella by the arm, he tied her to a post at the foot of the bed. La Croix knew not if he secured the captive, still dazed, for caution or because his wicked streak wanted her to bear witness. La Croix had never knowingly had a voyeur, and she knew not that she would have chosen Senorita Isabella.

His cock, slick with Isabella's juices, bobbed as he strode over to La Croix to assist with her boots. La Croix braced one leg against his shoulder as he pulled the boot off her other leg. After he had removed her boots, he inched off her stockings. He undid the buttons of her breeches and gently slid them down her legs, planting light kisses along the way. La Croix smirked at Isabella, who watched in dread and curiosity before turning away.

Settling himself between her legs as she remained in her chair, Harry inhaled deeply of her musk. Their gazes met, and she could feel ardor throbbing through her veins. She slid lower into the chair to provide him a better angle at her quim. He brought his hook between her thighs. That damn hook. She should tell him to remove it, but part of her liked being unsettled by it. With his hook, he nudged the rosy bud protruding from her nether folds, the cold metal a stark contrast to her hot flesh. He toyed with her a while till she nearly whimpered. He had an uncanny ability to know her thoughts, as if her body spoke to him in a language that even she was not privy to.

He replaced his hook with his tongue. She sighed at the delicious pressure, half noticing that Isabella was watching them once more. Gently, he licked her, spreading her folds with his fingers to open greater access to her clit. She moaned as he plied his tongue against her. Wetness trickled toward her anus and onto her chair. Damn. She would make him clean it later, along with the bedclothes stained with Isabella's blood.

He knew the spot that made her pant and

squirm with pleasure, relentlessly attacking it with tongue, then finger, then tongue. She gripped the armrests of her chair and strained toward her climax. As he devoured her with his mouth, he sank his fingers inside her wetness. His digits curled and stroked her inside, catapulting her toward ecstasy. She cried out as her hips bucked uncontrollably against him. He bore down harder on her clit, sucking till she wanted to scramble from his mouth. He pulled out his fingers. A spray of wetness followed. He agitated the fingers rapidly across her clit, making her want to crawl out of her own body, before shoving his fingers back in. He pulled out another stream of wetness, then went back to sucking her clit.

She lost count of how many times she ascended the peak. When he withdrew completely, the greedy part of her wanted him to continue, but she knew not that she could survive more.

Isabella had been staring agog at them. Harry smiled at her. "Want I should do that to you, *querida*?"

Her cheeks burned, and she turned away.

Bloody hell you will, La Croix wanted to say.

Before Harry could say more to the Spanish

beauty, Marinette grabbed his head and crushed her mouth to his. He had thicker lips than most men of his kind, though they were not as supple as those of men like Jonah or Baaku, but she enjoyed smothering his with her own. She sucked and bit his lips with the same fervor he had applied to her body moments before. She reached a hand down to his cock. Still hard. Hard for her. Or perhaps the influence of Isabella remained in his stiffness. What did she care whose cunnie he had rammed his cock into?

But she wanted to lay claim to this prize. This cock was hers. And only hers.

Rising from her chair, she kissed him harder and backed him toward the bed. She pushed him to sit down. Isabella kept her face turned away this time. She did not have to see, but she could not refrain from hearing.

Jealousy made her unkind, and as she sent the buttons of his waistcoat flying, she asked, "How many whores has your cock tasted?"

"Dozens," Harry answered, shrugging out of the waistcoat.

"And how many ladies of birth and standing?"

"Does that include our captive, Senorita El Chacón?"

He turned to look at Isabella. "She might have started as a lady when I entered her, but I have since made her a whore."

La Croix saw Isabella's eyes glisten with new tears.

"Does she not wish to watch?" La Croix mused aloud.

Standing, he went and yanked the sash from Isabella's gown. Shoving it between her lips, he tied her head to the bedpost then wound the sash over her forehead, securing her at an angle to view the bed in its entirety.

"You must watch all of it, *querida*," Harry told Isabella. "Lest you wish to join us. Do you?"

La Croix frowned. She had not permitted Harry to make such an invitation. Isabella did her best to shake her head.

"Perhaps you will feel differently later."

When Harry turned back to La Croix, she shoved him onto the bed.

He fell onto his back. Isabella looked on with pouting disapproval. La Croix climbed over him, straddling his hips. She positioned his mighty pole beneath her and set it between her dewy lips, hot and ready to take him. But his length made her start slow, chart a course for ultimate pleasure and

44

a long, slow journey.

She eased herself down, leaning forward and pressing her flattened palms against Harry's muscular chest. It rose and fell with his steady respiration. She had strong legs, able to hold her up halfway down his cock. His eyes blazed with desire, wanting to fill her. Slowly, she inched down his shaft, then back up again. She spread her legs to take him in further, lowering herself, muscles clenching as he began to fill her entirely, her engorged lips staking his cock as her own.

Frowning behind her gag, Isabella softly whimpered and pulled at her bonds in a futile attempt to escape. La Croix knew what she might be thinking—that while the dreadful negress was mounting Harry, she would have a chance to escape. But from the spark in the captive's eye, La Croix discerned that she was not dim of wit. Both women knew that escaping would do no good; Isabella would not get far, and any attempts would only incur their wrath.

La Croix ground faster and harder, her gaze upon Isabella, intrigued by her reactions, wanting to strengthen the woman's disgust, aroused by it even. The sight of the beauty bound before her drove her to tighten her muscles around Harry's broad beam, smashing her flesh into his pelvis. The pressure built hot and heavy through her body. Harry had started to move her, shoving her higher up the mountain of ecstasy. Soon, he grabbed her hips, dictating the pace with this thrusts. She strained toward her release. Within seconds, she would have it in her grasp.

Unexpectedly, Harry bumped her off of him. He pushed her onto her stomach, and turned her head so that she could see Isabella. Not ready for the position, La Croix tried to press herself up, but Harry pinned her head to the bed. He pulled up her hips and rammed himself into her. This was not how she wanted to be fucked, with Harry slamming his pelvis into her ass. How dare he make her appear helpless and dominated before their captive? But the angle of penetration was marvelous...

He slammed his hips at her, drilling his cock deeper into her cunnie. She cried out at the force of it. *Bloody bastard*. She saw Isabella's eyes widen as Harry pounded away. There was no relief for Harry held her in place. She had no choice but to feel the full force of his thrusts. She had a strong body, one that could withstand the assault, but even so, at times it felt as if he intended to crack her open. But she would not have Isabella believe that her feelings were anything other than those of pleasure.

When she thought she could take no more of his savage pounding, he slowed his pace, rolling his hips and sending flutters throughout her lower body. He reached around her hip and settled his hook between her folds, using the metal to caress her clit. She moaned in gratitude. As he fondled her with his hook, he alternated between gentle thrusts and a hard shove. It was exquisite to have his cock slamming into her, then have the kiss of his hook upon her clit. She wanted to move in rhythm with him but feared the wrong motion might cause the hook to nick her.

"I can tell you want just such a fucking," Harry said to Isabella, who shook her head vehemently. "Now that you're a whore, you'll want to beg me for it."

He rocked against Marinette with deliberation.

"I wonder what your father would think of his new whore–daughter? Will you tell him that you spent upon my cock? The cock of an Englishman? A pirate."

A new tear rolled down the young woman's

cheek.

Harry released La Croix head and grabbed her hip instead. She was close. So close to the end her body craved. He rocked their bodies together, growing the wave of bliss larger and larger till it finally engulfed her. She emitted a desperate wail as her body spasmed upon his cock. He sought his own pleasure now, banging away at her still quivering form. Abruptly, he pulled out of her and, fisting his cock, pumped his erection till his seed gushed forth, a few drops landing on Isabella's gown. He shuddered before collapsing onto the bed.

Marinette lay in the glow of her climax, her cunnie throbbing, little tremors fading from her limbs. She stared at Harry, unsure of how she felt. Ardor and jealousy had reduced to a simmer, but while she would welcome another fuck equal to what she had just received, anger toward Harry stayed her. She eyed him, his chest heaving with deep breaths, his hand about his cock soaked in seed. She crawled over to him and hovered her body over his. He opened his eyes to see her smile just before she brought her knee into his groin. With a roar, he doubled over.

She got off the bed. She had granted him his

revenge. She was now done with Isabella El Chacón.

CHAPTER SIX

Gunfire crackled over the deck of the *Bloody Baron*. La Croix waved her cutlass, sunlight flashing in glaring beams. She'd taken to polishing it to a fare-the-well, and she had her crew do the same. In a clear-day assault, the combined glare could have a blinding effect, a strategy of the Ancient Greeks.

It had been a fortnight and several days since she had ransomed Isabella to her father, and although the ransom and raid of Chacón's ship had brought in a good bounty, she preferred to put the episode behind her. Having had his revenge, Harry had been in good spirits, but she had no such satisfaction. Jealousy still simmered when she recalled how Harry had brought the Spanish beauty to spend. La Croix had thought that fucking Harry in front of Isabella a few more times might dispel her discontent, but it had not.

The Prosperity, a large merchantman, would suffer her caged wrath. The ship had at first attempted to outrun the *Bloody Baron*, which showed how foolish the captain was, for the tonnage of the merchantman was not the slightest match for the speed of the *Bloody Baron.*

British soldiers aboard *The Prosperity* hastened to reload their flintlocks as the sea breeze cleared the decks of the gun smoke. The *Bloody Baron* was near enough for La Croix to see the fear in some of their eyes, their scarlet coats making them visible targets.

She raised her pistol and fired, one of the merchant seamen dropping his rifle and staggering back but still alive and possibly dangerous. A second shot from behind her tore through the man's neck, putting him on flat on the deck. She turned, unsurprised to see that it was Harry who had delivered the deadly aim.

Harry shouted out, "Hook that mackerel, lads!"

The crew tossed out the boarding hooks, the *Bloody Baron* listing as they caught the masts and the railing, the wood creaking as the ships were pulled together.

La Croix's crew cheered as they threw the boarding planks over, pistols blazing, some men swinging from the masts with their swords. La Croix led the charge, blowing a black hole into the chest of an English sailor before flipping her emptied pistol around to use the handle as a cudgel. She swung it hard, cracking another man's skull at the forehead and sending him toppling to the deck.

Around her, Harry and the other crew members gave another good account, cutting their enemies down, their pistols and sabers and fists enough to lay *The Prosperity*'s crew low. Behind her, Harry swung the hook that took the place of his right hand, digging into the cheek of a British seaman and pulling hard, a stream of blood flying out of the man before Harry grabbed him and threw the poor bastard overboard.

One soldier got a good shot off at one of La Croix's men. He fell back, stunned, his blood soaking the sand and sawdust the sailors had laid down to absorb the gore and prevent other combatants from slipping.

The gunfire died down as there was now precious little time for reloading, but the clamor of the slaughter went on—men grunting and screaming, bones cracking, metal slicing through flesh, windpipes collapsing and choking out their last breaths. While most of the soldiers persisted, the sailors were less stalwart and began surrendering. A number of them cowered. Two had pissed their breeches.

"Gather up the rest of the crew," La Croix called out, "*The Prosperity* be ours!"

The men of her crew cheered and scurried to obey her commands. Around her, the crew of the *Baron* rounded up the surviving soldiers and sailors. Her three most fearsome crewmembers, including Baako, stood guard.

"Well done, my hell-hounds!" La Croix called out.

She knew the ship's captain by his uniform, a stout man with graying hair and a bitter sneer. She stepped up to him, bloodied cutlass in her hand. She raised the blade to his throat and said, "Present yourself to me."

He looked at her with disgust as his gaze took in her hair, which she wore in dozens of queues with shells woven into them. "I am Captain Nathan Cornwall. Know that Her Majesty's Royal Navy has no mercy for pirates. You will all hang from Gallow's Point."

"That may be," she scoffed, "but it shall not be this day. You need have more concern for your own life than mine at present."

A breeze wafted about her, and La Croix was

struck by the stench it carried, the smell of more than just sweaty and unwashed sailors. It smelled of death.

La merde.

Her heart sank. She had been on a ship with a similar stench before.

Jonah, a former slave who had joined her crew and proved a quick student of the seas, shouted, "Captain La Croix, come look!"

After leaving the captain and crew of *The Prosperity* to Piorer, La Croix and Harry followed Jonah and another crewmember down a ladder to the storage decks below. The stench worsened, the hot air thick in the ship's massive hull.

La Croix could hear their groans before she saw the first face, white eyes peering out of dark, black skin. She looked to be about ten and three years of age and was laying on a plank, hands and ankles shackled. Next to her, another African lay on the planks, his head by her ankles. Beyond him, another African huddled in chains, motionless, head lolling over the shackled ankles of the poor bastard next to him. They were lined up in that fashion from port to stern.

Rats crawled over them, and La Croix couldn't miss the numerous round, red bite marks against their dark skin.

Another shelf of captured Africans lay beneath them, covered with the dried urine and feces of those above. So low were the shelves that even a child could not sit upright. La Croix surveyed the massive hull, dozens of plank shelves filled with shackled negroes, moaning and crying and muttering in their native tongue, one she only vaguely recognized but did not understand. Her stomach churned.

She jumped when a hand reached out and grabbed her ankle. She stared down at a woman with barely any flesh between skin and bones. The woman spoke in a raspy voice, gesturing desperately to a little girl of three or four who lay beside her. La Croix pulled away, a vision of herself and her mother flashing through her mind.

Jonah came up to her with a lantern, and La Croix saw that the child lay deathly still, her breath near imperceptible. The mother continued to plead in a tongue La Croix would never fathom. Knowing nothing of her mother's tongue, La Croix instead spoke the language of her persecutors, French and English. Feeling disgusted with herself, La Croix turned her revulsion upon poor, powerless and pathetic woman before her. Did this woman assume that because La Croix shared the same sex or part blackamoor that she would wish to help her? This woman was of no concern to her.

"Fetch her water," she told Jonah. Then, feeling the need to retch, she scrambled back up the ladder and gulped in the ocean breeze. Guineamen abounded in the Atlantic, but she doubted she would ever become accustomed to them.

Before she was born, her own mother had made the journey from Africa, perhaps in a ship similar to this one. But her mother had never talked of the voyage that she and the other slaves had endured.

When she had collected herself, she went back to Captain Cornwall. "How many of these wretches below deck have you?"

The British captain stood erect, shoulders back and chest out. "About four hundred. They are the property of the Church of England and are expected at Codrington in Barbados."

"And they've sailed some weeks crammed below in the dark?"

"How else would you have them sail?" he sneered.

She drew out her dagger. "Would you prefer I slice off your cods?"

"How dare you speak to me in such fashion. You are a pirate and mongrel half-breed."

La Croix glanced over at Harry. "Perhaps he thinks my threat an empty one?"

"I am a Christian in the service of God and Queen," Cornwall declared. "I will not cower before the offspring of heathens, a whore who pretends to be a man."

Harry stepped into the captain and shoved his hook at the man's throat. "May I have the pleasure of draining the life from him and cutting him into tiny little pieces?"

Cornwall looked upon Harry with equal disgust. "An Englishman, are you? Serving a negress? I know not which is more despicable— you or the bitch."

Harry only grinned in response, his gaze pinned upon Cornwall as he spoke in a low voice to La Croix, "I could have a lot of fun with this one, Captain."

As could she. She had once severed a man's cock. But she had more questions.

"How does one speak to them?" she demanded.

"You are one of them," Cornwall replied. "You speak the devil's tongue."

Harry didn't wait for permission to slice his hook across the man's face. Cornwall screamed as he put a hand over the gash that ran from cheek to cheek.

One of the merchant sailors began to cry.

"Dear me, I meant to blind you," Harry drawled. "Fear not. I'll remedy that soon enough."

A young man dressed in the attire of his fellow white sailors stepped forward. "My name is Ekene. I translate."

"You aid and abet these white demons, do you?" La Croix threw at him.

Ekene lowered his gaze. "One must survive as best he can."

"Tell me, why are some of their faces charred and swollen?"

Ekene looked up. "There are some who refuse to eat, who would rather die of starvation. For that, they are burned."

"There is a woman with a sick child down there. Where is the ship's doctor?"

"He does not attend children."

"Why not?"

"If they are near to death or have a fever, it be

58

best to toss them overboard before they infect the rest."

During their exchange, Harry had broken Cornwall's nose into his knee. Blood streamed down the man's face, but her mind had only the vision of the young mother with the deathly child below. The woman's desperation rang in La Croix's ears.

Zut. She is not my concern, she told herself. None of the wretches were her concern. She was a pirate. A dreaded pirate. The daughter of the Baron La Croix. Her only aim in life was to amass as much bounty as she could and terrorize the sort of men who had made her what she was.

"Put Captain Cornwall and the crew into the rowboats," she instructed.

"Not before I break both his arms," Harry said.

"Don't be all day about it."

She frowned at the sound of bone cracking and Cornwall howling. She turned to Poirer. "Release the wretches."

He stared at her dumbly. "Release the wretches?"

"Undo their shackles."

"What for?"

"What for? To free them."

"But...are we not to sell them?"

Jonah came up to her. "I can sail them back."

"Sail them back?!"

Another crunch of bones preceded more agonized howling.

"Captain," Poirer said, "a healthy African can fetch forty British pounds a man. With more than four hundred of them, we'll not likely come across a bigger prize than this in all our lives."

La Croix paused, reconsidering. Who was she to care what happened to these wretches?

But she could not rid her mind of the girl and her mother. They would forever haunt her if she sold them as callously as her father had sold her mother.

"There be other fish in the sea," she said.

Poirer stood flabbergasted. "We ought to at least put it to a vote."

Anger rose within her. She wondered if he would so easily question her if she were a white male. "The *Bloody Baron* be *my* ship. You sail aboard it at *my* pleasure. That was the agreement made with my father before me, and me when I became Captain."

"But it is madness to turn away from such riches as these slaves will bring us! And Jonah alone cannot sail this ship. We've not enough men to spare for the journey."

Baako stepped forward. "I will sail with Jonah."

"Two men cannot make a crew."

"And I," offered Noah.

"We will make a crew of the wretches," La Croix declared, not wanting to send all her best men. She nodded at Ekene. "He will stay and translate the orders from Jonah and Baako."

"But—"

"Enough! We will take the captain's silver and whatever valuables we find."

She turned to Jonah, ignoring Poirer's dismay and the grumbling among her men. After she went through what Jonah would need to survive the return journey to Africa—it was not assured they would have enough supplies on hand to last them the trip, and they would have to mind the Royal Navy—she returned aboard to the *Bloody Baron*. She could not get off *The Prosperity* fast enough.

CHAPTER SEVEN

Leaning her head back against the chair, she cursed her past. She cursed her father for having sold her mother into slavery. She cursed the British for enslaving Africans. If she had not a slave's past, she would not have forsaken the slave ship. She would not have been so weak as to surrender to sensibilities. Now she had a discontented crew on her hand, and their disgruntlement would only grow if they did not find new prey to feast upon.

She had locked herself in her cabin without seeing *The Prosperity* sail away. Harry had knocked once upon her cabin door later that evening, but she had ignored him. She half wondered what he thought of her decision, then decided she did not care.

That night, she had helped herself to two flagons of ale, more than she had allowed herself to consume since her days with the Baron. When she had finally emerged from her cabin the following day, she overheard Dominic, one of the crewmembers, grousing about *The Prosperity*. Harry had turned around and decked the man. She noticed the man had made no move to retaliate. Her men never challenged Harry. A few had in Harry's early days as her slave. She could be as mad as Harry, do her best to intimidate and frighten, slice a man as if he were beefsteak, and still, as a woman, she would not have the same respect that he commanded. Even a black man fared better.

After a few days of seeing nothing but calm ocean waves and netting naught but a small fishing boat, she decided to head into Nassau and let the men drown their dissatisfaction in drink and wenches.

Most of her crew had already assembled in her favorite place of business in town, a tavern and inn that served also as a brothel, when La Croix entered. Francois, her boatswain, and Poirer were at a table with Dominic and Etienne. They stopped speaking as soon as she neared their table. She had no desire to drink with the men tonight and searched for Rosalina, a pretty Creole whom she always took to bed whenever she came into Nassau.

"Some rum, Captain?" Harry asked,

approaching her with a mug, "or would you prefer to find a room first?"

She looked past his knowing smile for she had spotted Rosalina between two sailors. Their gazes met.

"Not tonight," La Croix told Harry.

"No?"

She brushed past him, but he caught her arm.

"There be someone you favor over me?"

Not a man. She doubted she would favor a man over Harry. Perhaps there was no one, man or woman, she would prefer to have a tumble with. But that was precisely why she refused to bed him. Her preference for him was stronger than she liked. And the maudlin sentiments that swirled within her now needed the softer presence of a woman.

"Indeed," she replied, vexed that he would even present her with such a question.

She pulled her arm from his grasp and made her way over to Rosalina. Immediately, Rosalina left the two sailors, dashing their hopes.

"*La Capitana*," Rosalina greeted with genuine gladness.

"Have you a room?" La Croix asked her.

"For certain. I saw to it as soon as I heard the

Bloody Baron had been spotted."

La Croix smiled and followed Rosalina upstairs. Harry watched them leave, but she gave him not any acknowledgement, only noticing him out of the corners of her eyes..

Inside the room, La Croix wasted no time. She was already agitated from Harry's brief but potent touch. She pushed Rosalina up against the wall of the room, pressing her body hard against her. Her hand slid up over Rosalina's neck, gently choking her. The Creole beauty smiled back at her, knowing she meant her no real harm. La Croix's hand slid down the front of Rosalina's chest, crudely caressing her breasts though her gown as she covered Rosalina's mouth with hers. Their tongues entwined in a wet and sensual dance. La Croix pulled her away from the wall, spinning so her own back pressed up against it.

Moving her hands to Rosalina's shoulders, she unlocked her lips from Rosalina and pressed the woman down to her knees. Rosalina slid her hands along the sides of La Croix's body, her caress so much lighter than Harry's. Her expert hands made quick work of the breeches La Croix wore, peeling them down over her hips as La Croix directed Rosalina's head between her legs where wetness dripped.

Rosalina's tongue found La Croix's wet lips, taking in her scent as La Croix spread her legs further apart, before sliding down La Croix's warm crease to elicit a moan. Rosalina's hands wrapped around her naked arse and pulled La Croix toward her, her practiced tongue sliding down deeper until she found her slit. As with Harry, Rosalina knew the spots that La Croix preferred. She parted La Croix's moist lips, spreading them, revealing the pink flesh between. She slid her tongue up the front of La Croix, dancing across the sensitive skin as her fingers slid up inside of her.

La Croix let out a low growl. She thrust herself against Rosalina's fingers, wanting them deep inside of her, as deep as she wanted Harry's cock. Looking down, her stare met Rosalina's as the latter slid her tongue to her throbbing bud. She watched as Rosalina sucked it in between her silky lips, a third finger entering her hole at the same time. With patience and womanly gentleness, Rosalina attended her clitoris, pushing and pulling her fingers inside of La Croix. Her fingers were so much smaller than Harry's, her touch so much more tender. La Croix was glad for the contrast and, though her ardor did not flare as violently, she found herself lifted easily enough up the face of ecstasy. She thrust against Rosalina's hand and face toward her climax.

La Croix rode the wave, moaning loudly as the fingers inside of her continued to pulse in and out. She knew that Rosalina would continue to pleasure her until she stopped her, and once La Croix regained control of her body, she nudged Rosalina's head away from her. She missed her fingers as soon as they slid out of her but satisfied herself with Rosalina's mouth when it appeared in front of her, pulling her head close to her as she swallowed her tongue. La Croix could taste herself on the beauty's tongue, which stirred her still simmering lust.

"Undress," she said to her. "Those garments belong on the floor, not on your body."

Rosalina began to slowly undress in front of her.

"I don't want a show, *ma cheri*," La Croix said. "Off with them. And on the bed."

Dispensing with her slow dance, Rosalina quickly undid her corset, one that laced conveniently in front, and removed her skirt and petticoats. By the time she stepped out of her chemise, La Croix had also disrobed.

"Up on the bed," she said, her gaze taking in the soft curves of the beautiful Creole.

Rosalina wasted no time crawling onto the bed and reclining on her back. La Croix knew that the men she took to bed did not often attend to her pleasure. She wondered if that was why Rosalina preferred La Croix. That and her more generous coin purse.

Rosalina spread her legs to allow La Croix to settle between them. La Croix swirled her fingers in the dark down at Rosalina's mound before lowering her head to tongue Rosalina's wet slit. She slid her hands under Rosalina's rear, lifting her from the bed and pulling her to her mouth. Her tongue slowly opened the flower, petal by petal, tracing patterns up and down as the woman below her writhed on the mattress. Rosalina pushed her hips from the bed as La Croix's fingers slid inside of her easily, sinking into her hot wet flesh.

Rosalina moaned loudly and La Croix listened carefully, staring across Rosalina's chest into her eyes. She waited until she heard the lilt of her voice change and her breath quicken, then she withdrew her fingers, her hands moving to Rosalina's hips, twisting her body, rolling her onto her chest. La Croix's fingers slid down the crack of Rosalina's derriere as she pulled herself up lengthwise alongside her bedmate.

"Stay still," she whispered into Rosalina's ear as her fingers slid further down. One digit slid into her anus as the adjacent fingers sank back into her purse. "Slowly, push against my hand. I will tell you when you can spend."

La Croix felt Rosalina lift her hips, pushing them back, as she drove her fingers deeper inside of the woman. Rosalina moaned as La Croix deftly slid them in and out, twisting them to provide both pleasure and pain at the same time. She wanted to take Rosalina to the edge once more, but not push her over, controlling her in bed as she did all others around her.

"Very good, *ma cheri*. Like that. Now, faster." Rosalina's eyes belied her emotions, and La Croix stared into them, feeding off of them as she thrust into the whore. She wiggled the digit inside of her bottom. Rosalina groaned loudly, and La Croix smiled to herself. She controlled the very essence of the beauty now.

La Croix slid her fingers out. Rosalina's eyes opened, her hips still rising and falling. Two of La Croix's fingers dipped into Rosalina's dark hole, wiggling as they traveled deep inside.

"Look at me, *ma cherí*."

Rosalina stared into La Croix's eyes, lifting her hips as the fingers slid beyond where they had gone before.

"Now, fuck my hand. Fuck until you scream."

Rosalina's hips rose faster now, pressing back against the fingers buried in her cunnie.

"That's it. With haste!"

Rosalina's hips rose and fell onto the mattress, her breathing coming in short, rapid rasps, and her moans alternating between cries and moans. La Croix continued to impale her, waiting for the moment when Rosalina would reach her climax. After a few minutes, Rosalina's thrusting reached a fevered pitch as she finally rose to her knees, driving back against La Croix's hand and screaming as her body released the tension within.

Rosalina collapsed onto the bed and turned over, a large grin upon her red lips. La Croix crawled over her and buried her head in her large breasts, her tongue sliding up over one nipple as her hand pressed the flesh of the other orb. She pressed her knee into Rosalina's crotch, feeling her sopping flower pressing back against her. Rosalina felt so soft and rounded beneath her, unlike the hard planes of Harry. La Croix pressed her own wet crease down on Rosalina's thigh and humped her leg. La Croix knew it would not take long for her to reach her climax as she ground her body and rubbed against the Rosalina's supple flesh.

Rosalina matched La Croix's thrusts, pressing back against her, knowing the captain needed one more release before they were to settle into the night. Her moans matched La Croix's as they worked their bodies against one another. Pleasure built within La Croix and spilled over in a multitude of small, delightful tremors. Rosalina cried out soon after in similar release. Wet and spent, they lay curled in each other's arms.

"How I miss you when you are gone," Rosalina sighed as she traced one of La Croix's nipples with her forefinger. "Do you ever think the day will come when you no longer need the *Bloody Baron*?"

"Then how should I spend my time?" La Croix asked.

"You could spend it fucking me."

La Croix grinned.

"I worry of you," Rosalina said. "There is talk that the British tire of the pirates of New

Providence. They mean to send a governor to restore order."

"There is always such talk."

"And tonight, I heard of worse talk from your own men."

La Croix sighed. "They will despair a while over the slave ship, but once we find new quarry, they will rally."

"Will they? I heard Dominic speak of mutiny."

"Dominic is forever grousing. If it rains, he will grouse of being wet. If the sun shines, he will grouse of the heat."

"But Harry was among those discontented."

La Croix paused before asking, "What did he say?"

"I heard Poirer and Francois speak to him of a vote. When I neared, they lowered their voices, as if they knew—and feared—I might relay to you what they spoke."

"They risk themselves if they speak of disloyalty to Harry."

"Are you so certain of Harry's loyalty to you?"

La Croix considered all that had Harry had suffered at her hands: the menial and wretched tasks she made him undertake, the flogging she made him suffer, the paces she put him through in her bed. He took all of it without complaint, and rather than kill her when he had the chance or let her die at the hands of her enemies, he had chosen instead to slay her assailants.

But she never could be certain of his thoughts. He remained enigma mystery to her.

Nevertheless, although she was not pleased to hear that the displeasure among a few members of her crew had risen to talk of voting, she said to Rosalina, "If there is talk of mutiny, Harry will tell me."

"You trust him, then?"

La Croix mulled the question over. She supposed she did.

Though one should never trust a pirate.

CHAPTER EIGHT

The following evening, back aboard the *Bloody Baron*, La Croix knew in instant that something was amiss. Francois had a look of guilt about him, Poirer one of smugness, and Harry...Harry stared at her with his intensity. His gaze was often intense, as when desire was present, but she sensed no lust this time. She noticed Poirer had his hand upon his sword, as if he expected the need to defend himself. She immediately looked to her cutlass, which lay within easy reach upon her writing table. But would it do any good? She was outnumbered, and they had their weapons upon them. She turned her attention back to Harry, who stood in front of the other two.

It was the slave ship. They were still upset about the slave ship. But she had no wish to discuss it. What was done was done.

"There's been a vote," Harry stated.

She could barely contain the anger that surged at hearing his words. A vote? They took a vote?

"It would not have come about if..." Francois squirmed. "The men felt, you understand—"

"We lost two men in taking *The Prosperity*," Poirer said. "Three and ten were wounded."

She glared at him. "And they have been paid."

"And naught to show for our efforts. The same happened with that Matthews ship."

She dug her fingers into her palms. "I've served you well, have I not? The men have never starved, and I've been more than generous."

Francois nodded. "That you have, Captain."

"Then why was there a vote? What was the vote?" she demanded.

"The men voted for a new captain," Harry answered.

The hairs on her neck stood on end. After all these years, after all that she had done, all that she had sacrificed on their behalf... *Connards*, all of them.

"And who is the new captain?" she asked through gritted teeth, a part of her still in disbelief.

Harry smiled and bowed.

She stared at him in shock. Harry. Harry was the new captain. Her former slave. The man who had killed for her and saved her life. Of all people, he had turned on her? This could not be.

And yet, she should not truly have been surprised. Harry had no allegiances. He cared for nothing and no one. She had been foolish to think he might have cared for her in the least. Perhaps this had been his plan all along—to trick her into taking him as her slave, seduce her into letting down her guard and promoting him into a position that would make him fit for a captain. Now she understood why he accepted her abuse. Now he reaped the rewards of all his suffering.

Her fury had rendered her mute and immobile at first, but now that she understood his treachery and her own folly, she grabbed for her cutlass. But Harry caught her wrist and yanked the cutlass from her. He pulled her to his chest and brought the cutlass to her neck.

He turned to Poirer and Francois. "Inform the crew of their new captain. I have a score to settle with Captain La Croix."

Once Francois and Poirer left, she rammed her fist into his groin. For a second, he loosened his hold, allowing her to scramble away.

"You bloody bastard," she cried, quivering with emotion.

"Always been one," he responded.

Perhaps she would rather die than see the *Bloody Baron* fall into the hands of a mutineer. Too enraged to ponder reason, she lunged at him. He stepped aside. She flew by him, missing him. He shoved her into the wall, bruising her jaw. She scrambled safely out of his reach, then turned to face him once more. He cocked a grin and widened his stance, providing her a larger target. She accepted the invitation and hurled herself at him, intending to tear out his eyes or knee his cods, but he sidestepped her again, and she ran into her bed.

"Kill me, would you?" he asked.

This was fruitless. He toyed with her, like a cat would a mouse.

"As I should have done years ago," she spat

"Aye, that would've been the wiser course."

His patronizing agreement made her howl. She fisted her hands, wanting to punch him to a bloody pulp, but perhaps there was something better to bludgeon him with. She glanced about her cabin.

Seeing her thoughts, Harry calmly walked over to the sideboard, set the cutlass on top, opened a drawer and drew out the ropes she had used to bind him to her bed before. She paled. Was that the score he meant to settle?

"I'll kill you, I will," she warned him, "and happily spit upon your corpse."

Rope in hand, he sauntered toward her. "That may come to pass, but you'll settle your score in spades before then."

When he grew nearer, she dashed toward her cutlass on the sideboard, but he cut off her path. She made instead for the door. If she could find Noah or another crew member whom she knew would not have betrayed her...

But Harry tackled her to the ground. She fought him, which only seemed to amuse him. She managed to hit him across the face, which felt as if it might have hurt her knuckles more than him. He grabbed her throat, choking off her air with his tight grip. She clawed at his hand.

"Now is that the proper way to treat your captain?"

He continued to hold her down while rising to his knees. He released her throat only to put his foot down on her head, pressing the side of her face into the floor boards. Grabbing the rope he had dropped, he tied it around her right wrist. Pulling her to her feet, he dragged her over to the bed. She rained blows upon him while he secured the other end of the rope to a bedpost at the foot of her bed.

Her strikes seemed to have little effect. She might as well have been punching the carcass of a whale. She did catch him on the ear, and for that she received his elbow to the side of her head, blurring her vision and threatening her balance. While she tried to shake off the pain, he tied a second strand of rope about her other wrist and tied it to the opposing bedpost, stretching her arms across the width of the bed.

"Feel familiar?"

"You bloody *salaud*," she murmured.

"That be Captain Edge to you."

She returned a glare of hatred.

He cupped her chin. "Now address me properly."

She spat in his face. "Never."

He wiped her spittle from his cheek. She regretted her action, remembering how he had carved and scalped the harlot Molly. A muscle along his jaw rippled. "Suit yourself."

He pressed the tip of his hook into the center of her chest. She thought of impaling herself upon it, but that would likely lead to a slow and agonizing death. Perhaps that was what he intended. Payback for all the abuse she had made him endure. She closed her eyes and braced herself for a painful death.

Instead, her ears were met with the sound of fabric ripping as his hook sliced her shirt. She gasped, but she should not have been surprised. Of course he meant to torment her before he killed her. He hooked her breeches next and ripped the fall. She kicked him square in the shins, prompting him to go in search of more rope to tie her legs. With her legs and arms stretched to different corners, she was rendered powerless, unable to defend herself. He drew out his dagger and began to cut away at her garments: her coat, shirt, and breeches, leaving her in only her stockings and boots. He palmed a breast as he drew up before her, his breath heaving upon her. She resisted the desire to spit at him again.

He lightly pinched her right nipple. "Shall I give these as fair a turn as you gave me?"

She held his gaze, refusing to be cowed by him. "There be a special hell for for mutineers."

"I've already been to hell," he replied. "I've no fear of returning."

He gave her nipple a tweak before walking

over to the sideboard to retrieve the flogger she kept there.

Though she had not felt the tails since her childhood on a plantation, she resolved not to fear them. She would endure the lashes as Harry had.

"How many lashes did you have inflicted upon me?" he wondered aloud as he unfurled the tails.

Her pulse quickened as she considered the answer: over a hundred, easily. Likely over two hundred.

He whipped the flogger against the side of a breast. She inhaled sharply, but it had not been as painful as she thought. The flogger he wielded was the tamest she had, the tails being wide and flat. Since she had scarred his back with the knotted sort, she considered herself fortunate. For the moment.

He returned the flogger, lashing the side of her other breast. "Did you grant me any quarter?"

She said nothing as they both knew the answer. He flogged her breasts several more times, the last blow landing over her nipple and making her grunt. He warmed the rest of her body. When he struck her hips, the tails wrapped toward her rear, stinging her buttocks.

"I asked you a question," he said. "Did you

grant me quarter when I was your slave?"

He brought the flogger between her legs. She yelped, then answered, "I did not."

"It would be fair then for me to return the favor."

She grimaced when he slapped the tails again at her cunnie. He landed the flogger against her belly, her legs, her breasts with increasing strength. She strained against her bonds. She knew Harry too well. It was going to be a long night.

CHAPTER NINE

Harry paused the flogging to step to her. She trembled even before he touched her. With dread, she watched his hand reach between her thighs. His fingers connected with wetness. How was this possible? Horror replaced fury. Had her body been so conditioned to respond to him?

She struggled to escape his touch, but he moved his hand, and she only succeeded in rubbing herself against his fingers. He studied her reaction with interest.

"You understand now: your body belongs to me," he said.

Non. Non. Non. She could not be moved by this blaggard, this traitor.

But her body quivered as he continued to caress her, as gentle as a lover might.

The mutiny was damnable enough—now she had to suffer this? His arrogance needed no further propping. She had to resist. She imagined his head on a pike. She imagined cutting off his other hand. She imagined...his hard body slamming into hers.

I've gone bloody mad.

Her gaze met his, and she wasn't immediately able to hide her desperation. She needed him to stop fondling her, even if it helped to dull the bruising from the flogger.

"I know not two whores that can generate such wetness," Harry remarked.

She glared at him, but he rattled her composure when he curled two digits into her. Her legs shook, and she nearly whimpered. With calm and slow deliberation, he moved his thumb in concert over her clitoris with the stroking of his fingers. Ardor swirled in her belly, ignited by his ministrations. She avoided his stare while she did her best to suppress her rising lust. She must not give him the satisfaction of spending. Not after he had betrayed her. Could she truly be as weak as Isabella Chacón?

Resist, she commanded her body. But it was to no avail. Pleasure swelled from her loins, hardening her nipples, heating her body. And when he withdrew his hand, she wanted to plead for him to continue his fondling.

He instead resumed the flogging. She grunted

when he slapped the tails over her belly and cried out when he lashed it between her legs. Switching his hold to the other end of the handle, he brought the opposite end against the flesh between her legs. He rubbed the handle along her folds and clit, causing her wetness to increase. Her resistance faded to a sorry simmer. She closed her eyes, tempted to grind her flesh upon the flogger. He angled the handle at her slit and pushed. Her eyes flew open. Slowly, he pressed the handle into her cunnie. She could accommodate the girth of the handle, but its stiffness was disconcerting. She did not find it pleasurable at first.

"You'll keep it in place if you don't want my hook inside you," he warned, releasing the flogger.

She gripped the flogger as tightly as she could. Harry began to remove his clothes at a leisurely pace. When he was naked, he reached for her clit, strumming it while the flogger remained jammed up her cunnie.

"I want to hear you speak my name," he told her.

"*Foutu bâtard,*" she replied.

He put his mouth beside her ear. "Captain Edge."

Never!

He pushed the flogger deeper into her, alarm ringing through her if he meant to send it too far. He moved it in and out, fucking her with the handle. When he pulled it out, her cunnie felt raw. He propped a foot on the bed behind her, and his cock soon replaced the handle of the flogger. Compared the flogger, his cock was perfection, just the right amount of hardness. He rolled his hips into her, eliciting shivers of delight.

"You must call me 'Captain Edge' if you wish to spend."

"Fuck...you," she returned.

He grasped her jaw and tilted her gaze to his. Seeing the flame in his eyes, she could not swallow. She had sealed her fate.

He released her jaw and grabbed her hair, yanking it down to expose her throat. He seared his mouth there, taking large mouthfuls, sucking till her head swam. And then he shoved his hips into her, sending his cock high into her womb. He continued to pull her head back by her braids as he pounded mercilessly into her. She had enjoyed his rougher qualities till now. She did not mind pain and found it often enhanced pleasure. But the beating she now endured, without the promise of pleasure, was harder to take.

Speak the words he wants to hear, her body pleaded.

No, she would punish her body, punish it for betraying her. She refused to call him captain.

But knowing his stamina and after several minutes of feeling as if she might be battered into pieces, she uttered, "P-Please..."

He crushed his mouth over hers, kissing her so hard she would have yelped if her lips were not muffled by his. He withdrew and, grabbing his dagger, cut her bonds. He caught her before she crumpled to the floor and laid her on her back before tossing the dagger. He pulled her wrists above her head, pinned them with one hand, and reentered her. He thrust with as much force as before, but she was glad for the different position, and she was able to struggle against him, affording her a small amount of respite from the full force of his fucking.

He flipped her onto her stomach, her arse rounding the edge of the bed. She felt his shaft poking at her anus.

Mon dieu...

He sank into the tighter of her holes. She was grateful he did not ram himself in and that his cock was coated with her wetness. To her surprise, her ardor returned. His cock, filling her, stretching her, touching her in new places, caused the heat to spread within her. After he had filled her with his length, he bent one of her arms behind her back, holding it in place with his hook before he began thrusting in a more easy manner. He paused to play with her clit, and she nearly squealed in delight.

Then the devil returned. He smacked his hips into her arse hard. His vigorous thrusting made her teeth chatter. She could not keep up with the pumping, the pounding, the pulverizing. He unleashed his seed into her, filling her arse with his wet heat. She felt him shudder against the backs of her legs, felt his sweat drip onto her back. He slapped her buttock.

"You've a fine arse," he muttered.

When her body had recovered from the assault, she found desire still glowing within her. He had found his euphoric end. She wanted one as well. But Harry took the ropes that still dangled from her wrists and tied them to a bedpost.

He picked up his garments and put them back on before heading out, leaving her ardor disconcerted, her wits confused, and her hatred enlarged.

CHAPTER TEN

Tired from the pounding she had received, La Croix had chosen to rest instead of struggle against her bonds. She fell into a slumber and woke only when Harry sat down beside her upon the bed.

"I've a gift for you."

She fluttered her eyes open. She knew she wanted no gift from him. Sure enough, when she saw what he held, she stifled a groan.

It was an iron collar with a chain leash.

Resistance would be futile, and she had not the energy to fight him.

"I thought it would be fun to have *you* take a turn at being *my* slave," he explained.

Her entire body revolted at the thought.

"But then I decided that a pet would do," he finished.

No! She tried to pull away, but he pinned her down and closed the collar about her throat. She heard the click of a padlock.

She would see him burn for this!

He wrapped the chain about one of the bedposts and secured it with another padlock. He stuck the keys into his stocking.

"Most of the men are still ashore, and I mean to join them," he told her.

She wanted to dig her fingers into him and scrape the skin off his face.

"Dominic and Etienne will stand guard outside the cabin. Wouldn't want anyone to play with my pet without my knowing."

With a final smile, he took his leave. Left alone, she wondered if she might take advantage of his absence. But even if she could find a way to free herself from the collar, could she make it past two sentries? Could she scream? Surely not all her crew voted for Harry.

Even so, they might abide by the vote.

Tired, she lay down. She repeated thoughts of the many ways she would kill Harry before deciding she would need rest to have all her wits and strength about her. She had to be patient. She had to wait for the right moment.

In the middle of the night, a gunshot startled her awake. She heard a man calling, a few men running on deck, and scuffling sounds. But she could not determine what had happened. Perhaps one of the crewmembers, drunk, had fired off his pistol.

She lay awake afterward, unable to fall asleep as her mind recounted how all this had come to pass, how stupid she had been to make Harry her first mate when she could have killed him, how she should have known Poirer would betray her someday. She had seen the signs many times, but his loyalty to her father had blinded her to his faults.

Le con stupide!

She went though every man in her crew, assessing how they might have voted, and considered who she might trust the most. While it was true that Noah had once deserted her with the traitorous Delacroix, she did not completely blame the young man. He took his commands from Delacroix and could not have easily left Delacroix's ship. And having seen Noah's remorse, she doubted he would betray her a second time. If Jonah and Baako had still been with the *Bloody Baron*, the vote might not have come to pass.

But it was useless to pine for a past that did not exist. She needed to consider how she could escape, and if she needed to act sooner rather than later. Though Harry had made no mention of killing her, he might decide at any moment to dispense with her. Or maroon her on an island. She had to stave off such a fate. But how?

She had not gold to tempt him. At present, she had nothing. Nothing but her body. Her traitorous body that still craved his touch.

When Harry returned, kicked off his boots, and fell into bed, she pretended to be asleep, cross that he now claimed her bed as his. She heard him breathing deeply in slumber and wondered if she could hit him over the head somehow or strangle him with her leash if it were only strong enough. But with that damn hook of his, he would always have a weapon at the ready. He had tucked his precious pistol beneath his pillow, but she doubted it was loaded. Nevertheless, perhaps if he slept soundly enough...

As carefully as she could, she reached beneath his pillow while she kept her gaze upon Harry's profile, waiting for his eyes to open. They didn't. Not daring to breathe, she slid her hand further and touched the hard handle of the pistol. Perhaps she would be fortunate enough to find it loaded?

But in the next second, Harry's hand was about her arm.

"Now what are you about, pet?" he asked.

At first, she knew not what to say. He likely knew what she was attempting. Nevertheless, she told him, "You left me unfulfilled. I thought I might rouse your cock. Have you finish what you had started."

He didn't believe her, but he grinned. "Do you now?"

She looked toward his crotch. "I should like nothing more."

He released her arm, and she reached for where his cock lay beneath his breeches. She caressed the area till it hardened. Then she unbuttoned his fall to release his erection. She wrapped her other fist around him at mid-shaft, squeezing and pumping the bulk of its length, with a good deal more reaching up past her hand.

Bending down, she kissed and licked his swollen knob and the meaty shaft beneath it, blowing little streams of air onto its slick surface. His cock twitched as she wrapped her lips over her teeth and opened her mouth, tongue lowering to make enough room for him. His musk streamed up her nostrils, heady, intoxicating. She squeezed and pumped and licked and kissed, in and out while she opened her throat to take him in even further. One hand moved from his base to his sack, cradling those twin spheres while she worked his shaft even harder with her other hand. She pulled harder on that lever, while her other hand remained deft and gentle with its precious package. The contrast seemed to drive Harry wild. A flush spread across his chest, his muscles tensed, his eyes closed, a groan escaped his lips. She rubbed that wet wand over her face, nuzzling it, kissing it, worshiping it.

"Will you not pierce me with this mighty sword of yours?" she murmured.

"Now this be a fine turn," he said, amused. "All this time I thought you wanted to kill me, not fuck me."

She sat up to fondle herself between the legs. "Make me spend. I admit: nothing be more sublime than spending upon your cock."

He pulled her toward him but turned her around so that she faced away from him. Lifting her up by a buttock, he positioned his cock at her slit. She slid down his shaft, her mouth opening at the novel angle of his penetration.

He caressed her backside. "Fuck away then, pet."

It was true that he had left her unfulfilled, her

craving suspended in midair, unable to ascend and unwilling to descend. She wanted the ending that had been denied her earlier. She rocked herself up and down his cock, flexing her cunnie about him, relishing the way it throbbed inside her. To enhance her pleasure, she rubbed her clitoris. The dual pleasure felt bloody marvelous.

Worried that he might deny her once again, she pressed down harder, focusing all her attention on the need, the desire between her legs. Putting her other hand back, she braced herself against her arm and found more leverage to press herself against his length, feeling his cock rub the front wall of her cunnie. Amidst her pants and cries, she heard his grunts. He had begun thrusting, too, driving his cock deeper and harder inside her. The wall of ecstasy built fast and strong. She hurled herself at it, quaking as it crumbled down upon her. She nearly spasmed off his cock, but he held her in place as his wall crashed down with hers, his seed heating her cunnie.

She crumbled to the bed, the soreness in her legs creeping into her awareness as the euphoria faded. She was conscious, too, of the added fluids draining from between her legs. *The bloody saluad!* He had spent inside of her! But she had not the energy to address the matter at the moment.

As she allowed herself to drift into sleep, she determined that there would be plenty of time to kill Harry tomorrow.

CHAPTER ELEVEN

La Croix awoke in the morning to find herself alone in bed. She heard a knock at the door. It was Noah. His eyes widened to see her naked in bed. She pulled the bedclothes over herself. Aside from Harry, she had never before appeared naked before a member of her crew. Carrying a tray with a bowl of gruel and plate of biscuits, he set it beside the table. She studied him, misery plain on his face as he picked the weevils from the biscuits for her.

"I know you did not vote against me," she said.

He met her eyes. "Never, Captain."

"What was the vote? How many men voted against me?"

"It was done by ballot, though Poirer and Dominic spoke at length against you."

"Francois, too, I gather?"

"It is known to everyone that he follows Poirer."

"Who spoke in my favor?"

"I did. As did Sebastien."

"What of Harry?"

"He said nothing."

"I heard a gunshot ring out last night. What lout was playing about with firearms?"

Noah drew in a breath. "That was Francois. He blew out his brains."

La Croix's eyes widened. Had he such a guilty conscience?

"I said it might be a curse," Noah said with an impish sparkle in his eyes. "Said you might have cursed the men who voted against you."

"Did anyone believe you?"

"There are many inclined to think that those of us with black blood employ the black arts."

La Croix was grateful to Noah for the brief source of amusement in her ordeal. "Do you think you could procure me a weapon?"

"Done." Noah pulled out a dagger. "But you might need more than a dagger against Harry."

"I'll find an opportune moment." Taking the dagger, she hid it beneath the bed. "Do you think you could procure me a pistol as well?"

"I'll try. But if you manage to kill Harry, what then?"

"Do you think you could talk to those who

voted against Harry? Discover which of the men would be loyal enough to fight?"

Noah nodded.

"Then await my word."

Upon hearing footsteps, La Croix grabbed the biscuit and began eating. Noah took the tray and prepared to leave.

Harry walked in as Noah scurried out.

"I've another gift for you, my pet."

She frowned. Harry nodded, and Dominic entered carrying a cage they used for the livestock. He set it down in a corner.

"You'll sleep in here from now on," Harry explained. "Can't have you reaching for my pistol in the dead of night, seeing as how I keep it loaded."

Her eyes widened. Had she known this for certain, she would have made more of an effort to obtain it! Instead, she had slept away her chance.

Dominic flashed her grin before leaving. She vowed she would make him pay as much as the others. First Dominic. Then Poirer. She would save the greatest punishment for last. For dear old Harry.

Harry walked over and unlocked her, then dragged her over to the cage. She stared at in dread. The size of it was fine for a large hog or a sheep, but a grown human? She would have to bend her body to sleep in such a thing.

"Into the cage, my pet."

"But it be day, not night."

"You think I trust you enough to spare you more space to find a way to kill me?"

She stared at him agog. She was to be locked in this thing as if she were a common animal?

"What if I promise—?"

He laughed. "What? Promise not to kill me? You want to tell me what you and Noah talked of?"

She closed her mouth. He opened the cage door and nudged her in with his boot. After she reluctantly climbed in, he tossed in a chamber pot, then secured the door with a lock and returned the key to his stocking.

She spent the next few hours hour watching Harry go over supplies with the quartermaster and discussing with Poirer where to sail next.

"What is this I hear of witchcraft?" Harry asked of Poirer after they had rolled up the maps.

Poirer waved a dismissive hand. "Because of Francois. I explained Francois was simply weak. They think La Croix has the blood of witches in her on account of her mother."

"What think you?"

Poirer looked over at her. She flushed. She could not hate Harry more at the moment. To install her in a cage, naked, for anyone to gawk at, as they pleased.

"I knew her since she was but a girl," Poirer said. "Not once did she show she had any abilities with hexing."

The two men left. La Croix gazed toward the bed, where Noah's dagger now lay out of reach. To have a chance of accessing it, she would have to convince Harry to let her into his bed.

Her bed.

She heard commands being issued and the ship weigh anchor. She was thrown against the side of the cage as the ship pulled into the sea. A sense of dread filled her. In port, she had more friends. At sea, there were only the men who had conspired against her, and what men Noah might be able to rally to her defense.

Noah was her best hope. At one time, she would have placed all her hope in the likes of Harry. Now he was her greatest enemy.

CHAPTER TWELVE

Talk of witchcraft faded when the *Bloody Baron* came across a substantial prize, a merchantman carrying rum and molasses to the Carolinas. Her crew took its quarry, and Harry ordered several extra rounds of rum to celebrate. La Croix chafed at not having led the men to this victory, and she would never have provided her crew such vast quantities of rum all at once. A number of her men would easily drink to excess at every turn.

Harry celebrated by making her suck his cock through the cage. She had spent two and half days in the infernal thing. Harry would let her out to stretch her legs but only under his watchful eye. As if he knew that she and Noah had conspired together, they were not left alone since that first time. The dagger, however, remained beneath the bed. If she could convince him to fuck her in bed, he might fall into slumber without replacing her in the cage. Or she might beg him to let her sleep in the bed as the cage proved far too uncomfortable. Indeed, she slept fitfully, her body sore in places that had never ached before.

The night of the successful pillage, she readied herself for Harry. She fondled herself till she was wet. When he entered, he found her squirming in need, one hand between her thighs, the other groping a breast. His eyes immediately brightened with arousal. He removed his coat and weapons and leaned against the writing table to watch her. She lifted the hand between her legs to her mouth and sucked the moisture off her digits. He unbuttoned his fall and pulled out his cock.

"*Mon dieu*, I need a fuck," she told him.

He came over and unlocked the cage. She crawled out, heading to the side of the bed where the dagger lay, but he scooped her up and sat down in her chair, pulling her atop his lap.

"Would you not prefer the bed?" she asked.

"Perhaps later," he replied.

She rubbed her arse against his cock, till he lifted her and brought her down upon his hardened arousal. She moaned as his cock plunged into her. He palmed one breast while she groped the other. As she squirmed atop him, she plied her clitoris with her other hand. She prayed he would let her spend. Such exquisite sensations needed a proper conclusion. He bucked his pelvis up at her, slapping her arse. She stroked herself while his cock pumped delicious flutters through her loins. The end she yearned for was in sight.

He wrapped an arm around her waist to hold her in place while spasms shot through her. Her head fell back against him, and a cry tore from her throat. He bucked several more times. With a large, long groan, he emptied his ardor inside her. Once more, his mettle filled her. She scrambled off him, horrified.

"You let your seed in me again!" she screamed.

He rested his head against the back of the chair. "Merely marking what is mine. Are you afraid to bear my child?"

She trembled with fury. "I would carve it from my belly before I give birth to your bastard."

She looked to where the dagger lay, wondering if she could make a dash for it. But he followed her gaze.

"Something of importance there?" he inquired.

She lunged toward the bed, but he grabbed her and threw her in the opposite direction. He walked over and looked beneath the bed, finding the dagger.

"Now where did this come from?" he asked.

She remained mute, trying to assess the level of his anger.

"I would wager it to be young Noah," he guessed.

Her heart sank. What would he do to Noah?

Harry stuck the dagger into the top of the writing table.

"Back in the cage," he growled.

She crawled back in and spent the rest of the evening in the cage, listening to the crew sing and drink the night away. Her mind taunted her with visions of what Harry might do to Noah. Keelhaul the young man, flog him against the mizzenmast, make him eat the shit of the livestock before being roasted alive.

In the morning, she expected to hear of Noah's fate. Instead, she heard that Dominic and Etienne had had too much to drink and must have fallen overboard. They were discovered face down in the water.

Talk of a curse returned until they neared New Providence, where Harry planned to sell off the bounty they had captured. La Croix brightened. If the ship pulled into port, she might not need to rally her men for a fight—an unlikely prospect without Noah. She would need only to escape, then she could swim to shore.

The *Bloody Baron* did pull into port, but Harry did not let her out of the cage all day while he was on land. Food was brought to her by another crewmember instead of Noah.

When Harry returned, she feared to ask what might have become of Noah. Harry made no mention of Noah but seemed in rather good spirits. He had heard that his brother might be on the south side of the island.

And that was where they were to head.

CHAPTER THIRTEEN

D rake Edge had the same hard lines as Harry and stood a few inches taller. He had not Harry's icy blue eyes, however. Long, thick lashes graced eyes of dark cocoa. He also differed in manner of dress, with a red sash decorating his waist and jewelry about his fingers and neck. Light blinked off a large emerald ring upon one hand and gold chains rested upon his chest. One of the chains dangled a key.

"Are you always garbed like a peacock or should I be flattered?" Harry greeted.

Drake smirked. "Finally have a ship of your own, little brother?"

"Captain Edge to you."

With a snort and grin, Drake looked over the cabin. "This ship of yours be right impressive. She has some fine lines."

His eyes landed upon La Croix in her cage. "And what is this?"

"My pet," Harry answered.

Interest lighted Drake's eyes as he approached

her. "An uncommon looking wench."

"Have you never set eyes afore on Marinette La Croix?"

Drake looked sharply at Harry. "The she-captain be true?"

He returned his gaze to La Croix, who returned his study, trying to determine what manner of man he was. Did he bear affection toward Harry? Was he loyal to his brother? Did he possess the same bloodlust?

"Have you not heard the bounty on her head?"

"I thought it a rumor."

His stare took in every inch of her body, and a familiar hunger settled into his eyes. "But if she were a captain, how is she your pet?"

"Because he stole my ship," La Croix spat, curious to see how Drake would react. It would speak much to his character and whether he would prove friend or foe. "He be more lowly mutineer than captain."

Bending down, Harry yanked on the chain of her collar. "Did I give you leave to speak?"

"Be that true?" Drake asked.

"Aye, took her ship and made her my pet."

To her disappointment, there was no dismay or condemnation when Drake spoke. "I underestimated you, little brother. I would have wagered you more likely to be dead than to ever captain your own ship." He shook his head. "How did a negress ever become a captain and one worthy of a bounty?"

"The blood of the Baron La Croix runs through her veins."

Drake looked her over once more. "You fucked her yet?"

"What think you?"

They shared a chortle.

"And how do you favor dark flesh?"

"She be my first blackamoor, but her cunnie be as sweet as any I've had."

He fixed her with a stare that made her shiver.

"Your first, eh?" Drake murmured. "I've had at least a dozen mulattoes. It matters not how they appear to the eye but how they feel about your cock."

"You fuck sows and sheep as well, then?"

Drake laughed. "I would if that all be left."

Noah knocked and entered with a tray of tankards filled with rum. La Croix's heart leaped to see him still alive. To her further surprise, he appeared unscathed.

Drake grabbed a tankard. "Let us toast your

captaincy, little brother."

As the brothers raised their rum, La Croix exchanged glances with Noah. She wondered when her chance to speak to him might come.

"Let us dine aboard *The Curse of Neptune* in your honor," Drake said when they had downed their rum. "I have a cook who once served a Carolina plantation owner. We will feast like kings."

He turned to La Croix. "And bring your pet with you."

She frowned in dread. She had been in the man's company for but a few minutes. It was enough, however, to make her believe him more foe than friend.

*****

While Drake and Harry dined, they talked of their exploits and recounted memories of when they both sailed under Hornigold. Like a dog, La Croix sat upon the floor with a bowl of water beside Harry's chair. On occasion, he would feed her scraps, and she would have to take the food from his hand. Drake's cook was indeed skilled and had prepared a meal of quail, potatoes and meat pie. Not having eaten all day, she licked and sucked the juices from Harry's fingers.

"Drink," Harry told her, pushing her face into the water bowl while Drake looked on in amusement.

I will kill this bastard piece by piece over the course of a sennight, she promised herself as she lapped at the water.

She was only thankful that he had not paraded her naked onto *The Curse* and had allowed her a shirt and breeches. Perhaps he wanted to preserve her nudity for himself. But he had kept the collar about her, making her trail behind him like a *slave*.

"I see that you've your key still," Harry said at one point.

"It is always about me. Where is yours?"

"Buried safely on Tortuga."

Drake's voice darkened. "Buried? You do not keep the key with you?"

It was the first time La Croix had detected tension. Hitherto, she had determined there was friendship, if not brotherly affection, between them.

"As with you, I believed death likely to be my bedfellow any night," Harry replied.

"Where is the key buried?"

"In a cave on the leeward side of the island. The cave is fully visible only at low tide."

"You are certain the key has not washed away?"

"It is weighted to a cannonball buried five feet deep."

"And how will you recall the precise cave?"

"You want I should tell you so that you can access our treasure without me?"

"You know I would do no such thing," Drake growled. "As you can see, I have no need for those pieces of eight at present. And you?"

"Nor I, now that I have a ship of mine own and the bawdiest little pet to keep me entertained."

At that, Drake's mood lightened. They had slowed their eating. Drake sat back with a mug of ale and looked her over. "How about you let your dear older brother sample this treasure of yours?"

"There has been naught we've not shared," Harry acknowledged.

La Croix stiffened. Let another damned Englishman touch her? Another Edge?

"Then let us retire for the night."

She glared at Harry as he tugged on her chain leash. They left the dining room and entered the sleeping quarters. Drake sat on the edge of the bed with his mug of ale in hand.

"I liked your pet undressed," he remarked.

Harry nodded at her. Knowing what he expected, she pulled her shirt overhead. A small part of her enjoyed the appreciation in their eyes as they took in her breasts.

"I like that they do not hang like bags of sand," Drake said.

"The breeches," Harry said.

She had glanced about the cabin as she walked in and found little in the way of weapons except those strapped to the men. Even if she could get her hands on one, she was outnumbered. And she was aboard Drake's ship. There would be no friend here. She began to reconcile herself to the inevitable.

"And I half expected her to have a cock," Drake said after her breeches pooled at her feet.

"Why would you think that?" Harry asked.

"A woman pirate? I did not think such a thing existed."

"Captain La Croix be a rare gem."

She paused, surprised at not being referred to as his pet. Merely a slip of the tongue, no doubt.

Drake motioned to her. "Come hither."

Reluctantly, she went to stand before him and suppressed the urge to strike him when he groped a breast and then her groin.

"Aye, this one be all fair and soft," he assessed.

He palmed both breasts and rolled them atop her chest. Her nipples pebbled beneath his hands. He attached his mouth to one of the hardened buds and suckled. Was it the stimulation upon her body or the stare of Harry's that caused warmth to sprout in her loins? Unable to resist a glance at the tenting at his crotch, she wondered what manner of cock Drake possessed.

"It would seem my brother requires some tending to, pet," said Harry.

As she dropped to her knees, Drake revealed his pole. It was much thicker than Harry's. Drake slapped his cock against her face, and she decided the sooner he spent, the sooner the ordeal would be over with.

Drake groaned as she swallowed half of his shaft into her warm tunnel, her tongue wrapping around his shaft as she slowly fed him in and out.

"Her mouth be a right fine vessel," Drake said.

"I know I'll never tire of it," Harry agreed.

Drake's hand found the back of her head. He moved her on and off of his shaft slowly at first before pushing her down on him with greater force, driving his cock deep inside of her. He allowed her a gasp for breath before pressing back inside of her once more.

Harry stroked himself as he watched, then unbuttoned and dropped his breeches to hang about his knees. Standing by the bed, he pointed his erection at her.

"My cock needs tending to as well."

Grabbing her braids, he pulled her off Drake and shoved his tool in place. She swallowed him deep inside of her mouth, feeling the difference between the two brothers: Harry's length and Drake's girth. As he guided her mouth up and down his shaft, he reached down and grasped a nipple between his thumb and forefinger. He tugged upon the nipple, then used it to sway her breast from side to side. Wetness pooled between her legs.

Harry slid himself in and out of her mouth several more times before he let go of the back of her head and pulled himself out. Drake immediately took his brother's place. He bucked his hips at her face, pushing on her head so that her forehead smacked into his flesh and her nose was buried in his hairs.

"Your turn," he said before pulling out.

She was shoved onto Harry's cock before she could catch her breath. Spittle began to seep from the sides of her mouth, landing on her breasts when she had to switch back to Drake.

"I think your pet be partial to fat cock," Drake said, directing a smile at Harry.

When he shoved himself deep into her mouth, she tried to push against his thighs to prevent him from plunging his cock too deep.

"Bind her hands," Drake directed Harry. "Use the rope there."

Harry fetched the coil of rope hanging on the wall beside a pair of swords and pinioned her wrists behind her. When he was done, Drake was able to thrust as hard and deep as he wanted. She urged the spittle out of her mouth so that she did not choke on it, but his erratic rhythm often made her gag.

"Let us taste her other hole," he declared, picking her up and tossing her onto the bed.

He quickly shed his breeches and lay down on his back. He pulled her over him and pointed his cock at her slit. Curious to know how he would feel, she needed no prompting to slide down his shaft, encasing his thickness with her cunnie. She closed her eyes and shivered at being spread wide. When she opened her eyes, she found Harry staring at her. Would he be jealous if she enjoyed Drake's cock?

"Her cunnie takes me well," Drake said, slapping her breasts and pinching the nipples.

After playing with her orbs, he began to lift her up and down his length. Harry had been undressing and continued to remove his garments. When he was naked, he climbed into bed behind her. Reaching beneath her, between her and Drake, he collected the nectar there and applied it to his cock. He did this several times, then pushed her down onto Drake's chest. She felt the head of his cock at her other, tighter hole. And then he pushed in, pressing himself into her inch by slow inch. Drake assisted by pulling her arse cheeks apart. She moaned at the sensation of having both holes stretched. Once Harry had buried himself to the hilt, he began to thrust. Drake matched his rhythm. Her eyes rolled toward the back of her head as the thrill threatened to overwhelm her.

She never would have thought to find herself speared upon two cocks at once, tossed like a rag doll between two strong virulent bodies, her holes filled to the brim, drowning in a chorus of grunts, groans and the slapping of flesh. Her cry pierced the air as the tension within her imploded, shaking her to pieces as she came undone upon their cocks, which continued to spear her until Drake roared and flooded her with his hot stream. Moments later, Harry unloaded his seed into her arse.

"Damn, she be a fine fuck," Drake murmured after his cock had turned flaccid and slid from her.

Harry lay beside them to catch his breath. He pulled her to him, though Drake seemed reluctant to let her go.

"That she be," Harry acknowledged. "There be none finer."

She heard nothing but the sound of Drake's deep breaths in response, but she sensed that all was not rosy between the brothers.

CHAPTER FOURTEEN

D rake's dagger and pistol lay beside the bed upon the floor. The latter would do her no good as it was unlikely to be loaded, but if she could reach a dagger, she might be able to cut her bonds. She had spent the night lying naked upon the floor, fluids seeping from her quim and arsehole, struggling against the ropes that bound her ankles and wrists till they chafed and burned her, loosening only in the slightest.

"Wouldn't want you running away on us," Harry had said as he bound her ankles before departing.

She had wondered where he had intended to go in the middle of the night.

Drake lay snoring in bed, but Harry had gone off somewhere. She had to make haste as he might return at any moment. She inched her way toward the weapons, trying her best to move as quietly as possible across the hard floor. The wooden boards creaked a few times, but Drake remained asleep.

She prayed he slept heavily. Little by little, she drew closer. She let out a long breath when she reached her target. She had to turn on to her other side, facing the wall and away from the bed, as her hands were tied behind her back, in order to handle the dagger. Her heart leapt when she wrapped her fingers about it.

But her glory was short-lived. She cried out at the painful weight crushing her fingers.

"Tsk tsk," she heard Drake say.

He lifted his foot, and she inhaled sharply at the relief. For a second she worried that he had broken a finger, but she was able to move her digits after releasing the dagger.

Drake picked up his dagger and hauled her up by her hair. "Now what would you be wanting my dagger for, I wonder?"

He pressed the point of it to her throat. Her body wavered as she had not been able to ground her feet beneath her. She strained, leaning against Drake for support, desperate to maintain her balance so that she would not fall against the dagger.

"I've a use for you," he sneered, laying the blade against her head. "What say you to losing these mad queues of yours, eh?"

La Croix sucked in her breath. She was vain enough to care what happened to her hair. Her braids were a part of her identity, her gesture of obscenity to a world that would despise a woman and the bastard of a slave.

The blade moved along her scalp, pulling at one of the queues.

"Or, mayhap, we can trim the locks here."

He moved the dagger down her body, the cold steel grazing the contours of her breast, her midsection, before settling upon her upper thigh. He pushed her onto the bed and flipped her onto her back before returning the blade to the curls at the base of her pelvis.

"Indeed, I think a proper shave in order," he murmured as he brushed her curls.

He picked at a single hair and yanked it out.

Bloody saluad!

He met her gaze and smiled. He was worse than Harry, she realized. He grabbed several strands and sliced them close to her skin. Would he trouble himself not to cut her? Likely not. She remained as still as she could as he continued to trim her. She could feel the dagger scraping her, unsure if she should be glad or not that the blade was sharp rather than dull.

"You be a quiet one," he noted. "Are you afraid, love?"

She ground her teeth, preferring he not speak to her.

"Afraid that if my attention were to slip, I would nick you?"

Fucking saluad.

"But I would have you speak, my love. Did you have a fair time last night?"

Bloody fucking saluad.

She gasped when the dagger skimmed deeper. "Well?"

"I had a fair time," she managed through gritted teeth.

"Only a fair time?" Drake echoed with mock hurt. "Did my cock not satisfy?"

She knew the answer he sought but could not bring herself to respond right away. He sliced off more of her hair, then nicked her with the point of the dagger.

"Aye, it did," she ground out.

"You ever have cock as thick as mine?"

"Nay, I've not."

He grinned. "Be it better than Harry's?"

She hesitated. A part of her did enjoy how his stretched her, but Harry had better motion and perception. Or perhaps Drake was as capable as Harry and simply chose to fuck in a manner that best suited himself.

Knowing there was but one correct answer, she murmured, "Aye."

But Drake was not satisfied. "How much better?"

"A great deal better." *Saluad.*

"Prove it."

He had finished trimming her. Only the lightest of curls remained. She stared at him. Did he want her to extol the virtues of his cock?

"Your cock be of impressive girth," she tried.

He shook his head with exasperation. "I know that already. I want you to show me how much you like my cock, how much you desire it."

She frowned.

He slid the blade down her inner thigh and over her folds. "Seems I missed a few locks down here."

The edge of one blade now rested between her folds. She could barely catch her breath. Would he cut her down there? Could she bear it? Where the bloody hell was Harry?

The dagger moved along her flesh, prompting her to cry out, "I desire your cock more than anything!"

He cocked another grin at her. "Do you, love?"

"I do!"

He pursed his lips. "Do I believe you?"

"I was wet for you last night, was I not?"

"And now?"

She saw where this was headed. She hated that she had enjoyed his cock in part last night.

"Aye, I do."

"Do what?" He snickered.

She tried not to glare at him. "I want your cock."

"Do you now?" He nudged the blade against her.

When she got out of this alive, she promised herself that she would cut off his cock with a slow, dull blade. "Indeed. There be nothing I want more."

He moved the dagger and pressed the point of it to her. She had no means of defending herself. If she tried to push him away, she might cause more injury than if she did nothing. Was he cruel enough to slice her cunt?

She quickly said, unable to hide all of her panic, "I want your cock. I desire it. Will you not give it to me?"

To her relief, he drew back to wrap his free hand about his half hardened length. "You want I should give you this?"

"It be glorious."

As much as she loathed the man right now, she would gladly take his cock over the dagger.

"Should I let you have a taste of such a prize?"

"Just do, let me have a taste."

"Beg for it. As you are a wanton, desperate whore, beg for it."

"Please, please let me have your cock. I must have a taste of such magnificent meat."

He smirked in satisfaction.

"No drink, nor victual can best the taste of your cockmeat."

"Shall I fill your belly with my mettle?"

"I want it more than rum, more than wine."

He swept the clear viscous liquid seeping from his tip and brought it to her lips. A part of her wanted to retch, but she swept his fingers into her mouth and sucked hard, licking his digits as if starved. His gaze hardened, appearing half mesmerized by how ardently she sucked. He jammed his fingers deeper into her mouth, making her choke, before wiping his fingers against her cheek.

"I want more," she said, noting that he still held the dagger.

"Do you now, my naughty whore?"

In response, she licked her lips and opened her mouth, sticking out her tongue. He stared at the latter.

"My God," he breathed.

Tossing aside the dagger, he grabbed her by her braids and pulled her off the bed before shoving her to her knees. He presented his cock, purple with lust.

"As you have begged quite nicely for a whore, you may feast."

Not waiting for her to take him, he jammed his shaft into her mouth. She gagged at the sudden intrusion. He bucked his hips, allowing her no chance to calm her reflexes. Tears pressed into her eyes. She started to cough and convulse. When he realized he could not fuck her properly with her body in such revolt, he pulled out to provide her a much-needed reprieve.

Barely a second after she had collected herself, he shoved himself back in while pulling her face into his crotch. The hairs at his pelvis tickled her nose. When she started to gag again, he yanked her off him. One hand still fisted into her braids, he slapped his cock against her face with his other hand.

"Are we a happy whore now?" he asked.

"Yes," she mumbled.

He pushed his cock back between her lips and jabbed it at the inside of her cheek. He admired the protrusion at the side of her face. Pumping his hips, he fucked the side of her mouth as if he meant to pierce a hole through her cheek. After a while, he turned his efforts to ramming himself as deep into her throat as he could. He pulled her rapidly on and off his cock. She did her best to keep up, praying that he would spend soon. But he popped his cock out and stuffed his scrotum into her mouth.

"Suck my cods, my filthy wench."

She did as told. He grunted as she tugged upon the fragile balls inside his sack. With his thumb, he brushed away a tear that had slipped from her eye. "Tears of joy?"

He pulled out of her mouth and slapped her across the face when she made no response. "What was that, now?"

"Aye, they be tears of joy," she murmured, lowering her lashes so that he would not see the hate in her eyes.

"Why so joyful, love?"

"Because you have given me your cock."

"And you want more, I'll wager?"

Her sore and battered mouth wanted to scream, "No!" But she knew the correct answer.

"Aye, I wish for more."

He smiled. "Tell me, do all whores of your kind crave cock as much as you do?"

To refrain from glaring at him, she kept her focus at his groin. But he yanked her head back, forcing her to look up at him.

Bending down, he growled, "Do they?"

He gave her cheek a slap.

"They do not," she answered. "No whore relishes cock as much as I."

"As I am in a generous spirit, I shall grant you more of my cock."

He shoved his cock at her. As she was unprepared to receive it, his erection glanced off her nose.

"Now these I've never fucked before," he chuckled.

She immediately opened her mouth and sank down on his shaft. She had had enough of his play. She wanted him to spend and be done with her. She rubbed her tongue along the underside of his cock while she sucked hard enough to make her cheeks cave inward.

He groaned. "That be right good."

After swirling her tongue about him and sucking with all her might, she began to move up and down his length. He pressed his hand to the back of her head to push her further down his cock and faster. His groans grew louder, and she could feel him tensing. A few minutes later, he pulled out of her mouth and shot his seed over her face. Dollops of white landed on her lashes, cheeks, and lips. She could not be more thankful.

It was over, and she could turn her mind once more to her escape. The dagger lay upon the floor near the foot of the bed. Drake had fallen onto the bed, one hand holding his softening cock and looking as if he might return to the stupor of sleep. Perhaps she would have another chance at the dagger.

But then Harry walked in.

CHAPTER FIFTEEN

"What have you done to my pet?" Harry demanded. Unlike Drake, he was mostly dressed. He had on his boots, breeches and a shirt.

Drake pried open an eye. "Improved her."

Harry stared at what was left of the bush at her mound. "Not bad, I suppose, but ye would make for a bloody poor barber."

Drake chortled. "I decorated her for you too."

Harry wiped the mettle coating her eye. She was glad that Drake's seed no longer filled her vision.

"Did I allow that you could touch her without my say?" asked Harry, half in jest, half serious.

"She begged dearly for my cock."

She dreaded what Drake would say next.

As she expected, Drake added, "Declared my cock the best she's ever had."

Harry neither smiled nor frowned, but it seemed his jaw tightened ever so slightly as he looked upon his brother.

To ensure that Harry understood how the statement applied to him, Drake said, "Better than yours, Harry."

Harry turned his gaze from Drake to her. He seemed to expect such taunting from Drake but was not amused. "Is that so?"

If she refuted Drake's words, she would incur the older brother's wrath. Remaining silent might incur Harry's wrath. Which did she prefer?

Harry gripped her chin and a tight grasp. "Do you indeed prefer my brother's cock?"

"I would have both of yours," she answered.

"But you desire his more?"

She glanced over at Drake. He still appeared lethargic, satiated. Harry, however, was not. He was likely to be more angry at the moment.

"Yours," she said.

"I'm not sure I believe you."

"It is your cock I shall always desire. Yours I want to fuck."

"In what manner?"

"In all manners. With all parts of my body." She could see a bulge forming in his breeches. There would be no chance of escape until Harry was satisfied, too.

"I crave it," she continued, "I should be

miserable an' you not let me have it."

"Are you wet for my cock now?"

To her surprise, she was. Slipping his hand between her thighs, Harry drew out new wetness.

"That be from me," Drake said.

"Is that true, pet?" Harry inquired of her.

She shook her head. "Nay, 'tis yours. 'Tis all for you... Please give me your cock. Please fuck me."

He unbuttoned his fall and pulled out his shaft. "Make it as hard as possible."

She suppressed a groan. Her mouth and throat felt raw from Drake. The last thing she wanted was to swallow more cockmeat, but she dare not defy Harry's orders. Dutifully, she wrapped her lips about him. His lashes fluttered when she sucked.

"There be a good pet," he murmured.

As it had been with Drake, with her hands bound behind her, her movement up and down his cock was limited. Harry placed the flat of his hook behind her head to guide her deeper and faster onto him. She took in as much of him as she could, feeling warmth building in her loins. What was it about Harry's cock that had such an effect upon her, even when she wanted to see him dead?

Within a minute, his cock was as stiff as a maypole, a slick and delicious velvet hardness. Her cunnie flexed in hopeful anticipation. He pounded her mouth a little while longer before pulling out. He looked over at Drake.

"We may never know for certain whose cock she prefers," he said, "but it would be quite obvious which cock betwixt us can make her scream more."

Dismay and anticipation flooded her. She wanted Harry's cock in her aching cunnie, but she could not be sure what he intended.

"You want a challenge?" Drake asked, perking up.

This did not bode well, she decided.

At the foot of Drake's bed was a low, upholstered bedside bench. Harry hooked his foot around one of the legs and dragged it over. He pulled her over the bench and pushed her onto her breasts and knees, then stood behind her. He spanked his shaft on her derriere.

"Hold your position, pet, or you'll have my hook in your arse," he warned her.

She felt the prod of his cock before it sank into her cunnie.

"A mighty fine slut," he murmured. "Always

wet for me."

Her cheeks burned at the unfortunate truth. Not only was she wet, but her arousal bloomed as he sawed his cock in and out of her. The stroking of her insides stirred the tension, the need. Her clitoris screamed for attention.

"Do you wish you could touch yourself, pet?" he asked.

She made no response, but he untied her wrists.

"Touch yourself," he commanded.

Eagerly, she reached between her thighs and rubbed herself.

"My God, she is a wanton creature," Drake murmured as he idly caressed his cock.

She heard the smile in Harry's voice. "That she is."

A part of her was tempted to cry. How was it that she was such a slut for them? But she would never let them see her cry, never let them see they could make her miserable. After she cut off their cocks, she would bake their flesh and eat it.

Harry delved deeper into her, but she did not mind the roughness while she could fondle herself. Little by little, his thrusts pushed her toward the edge of the bench. Deciding he needed a better hold on her, he picked up the sash he had discarded last night and tied it around her waist. He hooked the sash and was able to hold her in place as he rammed his cock into her, jarring her teeth and making her cry out.

"Surely you can do better than that," Drake scoffed.

Harry planted one foot beside her on the bench, giving him more leverage to pound her with even greater force. She felt as if her teeth might chatter out of her head.

"Ahhh!" she exclaimed when his pelvis slammed into her arse.

"Beg for more, my pet."

Nay. That was the last thing she wanted.

"Beg," Harry ordered.

She drew in a ragged breath and muttered, "More, please."

"Good pet."

He drilled into her fast and furious. She had ceased fondling herself, intent only on bracing herself against the blows, her body desperately trying to find an extra half inch—quarter of an inch—further away from him. Tears pressed against her eyes as each thrust sent pain shooting through her from the inside out. Her throat began to turn hoarse from her cries.

"Impressive," Drake allowed, hopping off the bed and coming round to stand in front of her, holding his half-hardened cock.

Cupping her chin, he titled her head up, pausing to admire the glisten of tears in her eyes before shoving his member at her mouth. Unprepared to swallow him, she choked, but he continue to push himself in. At least Harry had ceased thrusting while she attempted to take Drake's cock. Once she had adjusted, Harry resumed, driving her face into Drake's crotch. Drake put a hand to the back of her head, attempting to smash her face into his groin as much as possible before shoving her back toward Harry. At first, they synchronized their motions, their bodies buffeting her like waves on either side of a ship. But their efforts did not last long, and their rhythm grew erratic, at times plunging into her at the same time. She thought her body might fold, forced to crumble between them.

"My turn," Drake declared.

Harry withdrew, and she collapsed onto the bench. Her body, tossed to and fro, possessed only the strength of a rag doll. Drake picked her up and tossed her onto the bed. She landed on her back.

He pulled her till her arse was halfway off the edge. He pushed her legs up till her knees knocked into her breasts, then plunged himself into her.

"God, what a bloody fine cunnie," he murmured to himself.

He grabbed her hips and drilled his cock into her. As with Harry, there was no escape for her body, no space or angle for relief. In fact, she found her present position more difficult.

"I made her scream far louder," Harry commented, though her cries and the smacking of flesh against flesh filled the room.

Not to be outdone by his younger brother, Drake clamped down harder upon her and slammed so hard into her she prayed she would faint.

But she didn't. She grabbed his wrists and dug her fingers into him, trying to loosen his hold or distract him. The bed creaked with the force of his hammering, and she doubted it would hold.

The flush about Drake's chest and throat deepened. He favored quick rather than deep thrusts. Perspiration dripped from his head onto the back of her legs. Cursing through his teeth, he bucked wildly against her as liquid heat filled her.

He trembled and shook, his eyes rolling toward the back of his head, before he finally stumbled from her and fell into the bed. Silently, she thanked the Lord.

"Now watch this," Harry said, taking Drake's place.

Mon Dieu. Non.

She could take no more. Her body felt too battered.

Harry rubbed his shaft along the wetness of her flesh, then sank into her arsehole. Dread filled her. She could not taking a beating there.

Drake watched as Harry rubbed this thumb over her clit while sliding himself in and out of her arse. Still reeling from the pommeling she had received at their cocks, her body became desperate for pleasure to wash away the pain. His caresses upon her clit were like water to a wanderer in the desert. She latched onto the sweet sensations, nurturing them with her attentions, hoping the embers would not take long to burst into flame.

Her prayers were answered as arousal found lightness in the dark. Her former screams now became sighs and groans, squeals of joy. Though Harry was absolutely capable of such cruelty as to dash the water from her lips before she could drink, her body could not resist the temptation. It would go down the more dangerous path. Her lust would not be denied.

And when Harry curled his digits inside her, she could have cried at the glory of the sensations. The earlier pain became a springboard that sent her hurtling to new heights. His thumb on her clitoris, his fingers in her quim, his cock in her arse. The coil of tension inside her sprang, letting forth a fountain of wetness. Pulling out his fingers, he spread the moisture over her bud and folds with quick brushes of his hand before plunging his digits back in and pulling out another spray of her wetness.

"S'blood," Drake murmured in awe.

Intent on his own finish now, Harry wrapped his hand about her throat. He bucked his hips at her, sending his cock deeper into her rectum. The highs of her climax combined with the reduced flow of air made the room about her spin. She half expected him to choke her to death. His hand did close more tightly about her as he spent, but after pumping his seed into her arse, his body relaxed. She gasped for breath and curled away from him to allow her legs to fall onto the bed.

With her eyes closed, she reminded herself of the revenge she would exact, how she would make them pay for every bruise, every drop of seed, even second of pain, and even every moment of pleasure.

She heard footsteps and prayed that Drake and Harry would not invite a third person into their party. Her body had yet to recover.

"Captain Edge!" she heard one of her crewmembers call from behind the door. "Captain Edge."

With a grumble, Harry buttoned his fall and strode over. He opened the door and glared at the man. "This had better be bloody important for you to come disturb me at such an hour."

"Captain Edge, Poirer is dead!"

CHAPTER SIXTEEN

"Poirer dead?" Harry grumbled as if vexed that Noah would disturb him with such news.

"Traverse spotted him through the spyglass, hanging from a tree," Noah said. "It was a ghastly sight, Traverse said, for it would seem someone had sliced Poirer a dozen times and cut out his eye and tongue. There be talk of curses, Captain. The men are afeared."

Harry snorted. "I will speak to them."

Noah glanced briefly at La Croix before following Harry, leaving her alone with Drake.

To her relief, Drake dressed himself, and, perhaps curious to see the sight Noah had described, left the cabin.

For a second, she could hardly believe her luck. In the next, she hopped over to the wall where a sabre hung. She knocked it off with her shoulder. It clattered to the floor, but Drake did not return. She opened a drawer of a sideboard, picked up the sabre, and put it with the blade sticking out of the drawer before shutting it in place. Fitting her wrists over the sabre, she rubbed her bindings against the blade till it cut through enough of the rope for her to pull free.

After untying her ankles, she grabbed a shirt and breeches from Drake's wardrobe. She used one of the ropes to tie the breeches in place, then grabbed the sabre. Her heart pounded as she opened the cabin door.

No one confronted her. Drake had only a few men aboard as most of his men were in port, likely sleeping after spending the night three sheets to the wind. She wondered how many of her crew were with Drake's men. Even if she had more friends than enemies aboard the *Bloody Baron,* she had better make for land and find her way to Nassau.

"Now, what have we here?" one of Drake's crewmen asked as she rounded the corner of the cabin.

Without hesitation, she drove her sabre into him, but before she could pull it back out, an arm encircled her neck and pulled her away. She swung her elbow back as hard as she could, delivering a blow to her assailant's midsection. He grunted but kept his arm about her.

"I'll have no more of that," Drake said, pointing his dagger at her face. He yanked her even closer to him. "And I thought you a better behaved pet than that. Mayhap Harry did not train you well enough, but I will prove a better Master. Would you like that, love?"

He caressed her jaw with his thumb. "How would you like my fat cock every night instead of Harry's? Eh? I'll have that cunnie of yours stretched as wide as the Atlantic."

She glanced over at the *Bloody Baron* and saw that Harry was heading back to *The Curse of Neptune*. She felt confident that her prospects with Drake would prove no better than what they were with Harry.

"I think not," she muttered.

"No? You prefer a cripple?" he asked with an edge to his voice. He tightened his hold around her neck as if he meant to choke her. "Perhaps you need to learn what a man with two proper hands is capable of."

Harry climbed over the bulwark and stepped onto deck. He looked surprised to see her and Drake.

"Ah, Harry," Drake said. "I've decided that I'll be on my way to Florida."

Harry said nothing.

"And I'm taking your pet with me."

"I did not intend her a gift," Harry replied coldly.

"No? Not even for your brother whom you've not set eyes on in years?"

"You could have come back for me in Cuba. You didn't."

"I thought you dead. You were in the hands of Governor Chacón, and he would not have allowed you to live. But if you'll not gift me this pet of yours, I'll pay for her."

"I'm not selling."

Drake's body tensed. A small part of her was gratified that Harry had no wish to part with her.

"There be plenty of other black cunnie to be had," Drake drawled.

"You always wanted what was mine. Since we were boys. And you never asked. You only took."

Drake grinned. "I was a proper older brother."

"I'm not letting you take her. I would sooner neither of us have her than see you run off with what is mine."

Harry took out his pistol and calmly loaded it.

She started to struggle desperately against Drake. This was not how she wanted to die, without a chance to defend herself.

Drake snorted. "Pity to kill such fine cunnie over jealousy."

Harry took aim. "It would be a pity."

Mon dieu! She pulled and yanked at Drake, but he held fast.

"You're bluffing," Drake threw at Harry.

"Am I?"

La Croix closed her eyes. This, then, was the end. She hoped he would at least spare her a quick death.

He pulled the trigger.

Blood sprayed from her head.

To her surprise, she felt no pain, not the scald of iron nor the crack of bones in her face.

She took in a breath as Drake's arm slid away.

She released her breath. She could breathe still. She opened her eyes. She could see, perfectly, save for the drops of blood on her lashes. And she was able to stand on her own. Her life was not draining from her. Turning around, she saw Drake fall to the deck, half his face blown away.

Harry had missed! He had shot his own brother instead!

She had no time to rejoice at such luck. She grabbed the dagger from Drake's hand to face Harry.

Though his brow furrowed in slight disconcertion, he seemed as surprised as he had been when Noah informed him of Poirer's demise, a grim and savage death. Of the kind that Harry would inflict...

Harry reloaded his pistol. She frowned. Now he meant to correct his aim, and the meager dagger she held would be no match for his firearm.

Two of Drake's men, having undoubtedly heard the gunshot, appeared. Harry fired his pistol into the stomach of one while she tossed her dagger into the other. Now she was without a weapon to confront Harry.

Suddenly the bell aboard the *Bloody Baron* rang.

"Frigate!"

She and Harry both turned toward the sea to see a ship that must have been lurking just outside the cove behind a rocky cliff. A cannonball splashed within fifty yards of them.

"You best get aboard the *Bloody Baron*," Harry told her as he poured gunpowder into his pistol once again. "The men await your command."

Perplexed, she blinked several times. Had she heard him correctly?

"We took another vote," he explained, jamming the bullet into the barrel. "They want no more of your curse."

"My curse?"

"I told them the next man may fare even worse than Poirer."

She eyed Harry intently. He did not seem disturbed by her curse. Nor that Poirer was dead, following the deaths of Dominic and Etienne, who had drowned because Harry had allowed the men too much to drink. And then there was Francois, who had eaten his own gun while she was tied in Harry's cabin, alone while Harry had gone off to...what had Harry gone off to do that night?

She started. Had Harry...all this time?

But she had little time to reflect for the frigate launched another cannonball at them.

"Captain La Croix!" Noah called from the *Bloody Baron.*

Harry strode over to Drake and yanked the chain with the key from his neck. He handed it to La Croix.

"The treasure be buried in the highest cave on

the leeward side of Tortuga," he said. "In the fifth cave to its left, five feet in, five feet down, you'll find my key."

She looked at him in disbelief.

"Sail the *Baron*," he told her. "I'll take care of the frigate."

When she did not move, he barked, "Now!"

She hopped into the rowboat he had taken between the ships. Noah awaited her and assisted her onto her ship.

"It be the British Royal Navy," he explained of the frigate, "with two more behind her."

"Ready the cannons and hoist the sails," she ordered.

"Aye, Captain."

Had she time, she would have relished the sound of his words. The *Bloody Baron* was hers once more.

With the frigate closer, the *Bloody Baron* exchanged cannon fire. She glanced over at Drake's ship, expecting they would engage as well. Instead, she saw Harry rolling a keg of gunpowder up to another keg. She turned her focus to escape. Unless the frigate took out a sail, the *Bloody Baron* would win the battle of speed.

When next she looked over at *The Curse of*

Neptune, she saw Harry at the ship's wheel, turning the bow of the ship at the frigate. He had assembled several kegs on deck. She thought of slowing and seeing if her cannons could damage the frigate enough to allow both of them to escape, but with the other two frigates approaching, she could not take the chance of lingering. Another round of cannon fire from the frigate splintered part of the bulwark and took out a jib.

But faced with *The Curse of Neptune* baring down on her, the frigate turned its cannons away from the *Bloody Baron*. She saw Harry still at the wheel, now with a torch in hand. She narrowed her eyes. Did he mean to set the ship on fire?

He did, she realized as *The Curse of Neptune* drew closer and closer to the frigate. The frigate fired her cannons, taking out the mizzenmast, but it was too late. She watched as Harry tossed the torch toward the collected kegs of gunpowder. *The Curse of Neptune* rammed into the side of the frigate as an explosion of fire engulfed both ships.

"Harry!" she gasped, scrambling from the poop deck to the lower deck. She grabbed the spyglass from Noah to scan for signs of life. But she could see nothing in the inferno but the flames.

"Captain, the other frigates," Noah reminded her, as if he knew she contemplated whether to turn the *Bloody Baron* around to search for survivors.

She nodded. She stood at the bulwark and watched the fire consume the frigate and *The Curse of Neptune.* The other two frigates chose not to give chase and instead went to the aid of its fellow ship.

Only when they were safely out to sea, long past when she could see the lines of the cove, did La Croix stir.

"Captain, 'tis good to have you back," Noah said.

"Did...did Harry lay the deaths of Poirer and the others at my feet?" she asked.

"I spoke first of a curse the night Francois died."

"He didn't kill himself, did he?"

"Nay."

"And Dominic and Etienne? Did they drown with Harry's help?"

"And mine. They were mighty drunk, and tossing them over was child's play. But Harry wanted Poirer all for himself."

151

She shook her head. It was still too much to comprehend.

"But Harry voted for the mutiny, did he not?"

"I reckon he had to, Captain."

She rubbed her temple. But if Harry had had plans to undermine the mutiny, why did he not speak of it to her? Had the bloody bastard wanted to avenge all that she had done to him in bed?

She supposed she would never know.

Still conflicted, she knew not whether to curse him or thank him. She looked down at the key he had put in her hand. When she reached Nassau, on the other side of the island, she and Rosalina would make their way to Tortuga and unearth the treasure. Then she might take a respite from piracy for a while.

Perhaps. She did just get the *Bloody Baron* back, after all.

She closed her eyes to feel the press of air against her face, and enjoy the sound of sail snapping in the wind, her favorite form of music.

"She be a right fine vessel, this ship of yours," Noah said.

Opening her eyes, she turned to him. "Aye, and she be in need of a first mate."

Noah raised his brows. "Captain?"

Humble and pious, for a pirate, Noah differed from Harry in many ways, but she valued his loyalty and seamanship. He had not the complicated layers that Harry possessed.

As if she could still see *The Curse of the Neptune*, she looked back toward New Providence. The makings of sorrow began to set into her heart, though her anger with Harry, even knowing he had sacrificed his life for hers, had yet to dissipate. She knew—and should be relieved—to never meet another pirate like Harry Edge.

He could not be trusted to be kind of heart, but neither could he be trusted to be traitorous. She hated him. She admired him. He had taken her body to rapturous heights and drowned her soul in darkness. With Harry, she felt thrown upon waves that were all at once stormy, thrilling, violent, and overwhelming.

La Croix turned toward the horizon, ready for calmer, less wicked seas.

Thank you for taking this dark and wicked voyage with me! If you enjoyed the tale, please consider leaving a review.

Much obliged,
Em

GET A FREE BOOK

Simply go to
www.iheartsteamyromance.com

OTHER WORKS BY EM BROWN

51641329R00093